Chapter One

CHARLES PARIS LOOKED out from the bar of the Pinero Theatre, Warminster, over the gathering September twilight, and felt mildly guilty that he wasn't really listening to what Gavin Scholes was saying. The warmth of the third large Bell's and the glow of being in work cocooned him and he only caught the occasional word of the director's exposition of *Macbeth*.

"For me, Charles, it's the tragedy of an unimaginative man, whose imagination, which has for so long lain dormant, is suddenly awakened. And he doesn't know how to cope with this new dimension in his life."

"Ah."

"Don't you see it that way?"

"Well, er . . ."

"So, I mean, the Weird Sisters . . . well, they just knock him sideways. His mind's kind of invaded by these alien thoughts that he can't understand. You know, 'there are more things in heaven and earth than are dreamt of in your philosophy' . . ."

"Surely that's *Hamlet*, isn't it?"

"Erm . . . yes, of course it is, but I always think that in approaching a Shakespeare, one has to think in terms of the Complete Works."

"Ah."

"Each play is just another facet of the sparkling diamond that was Shakespeare's Genius. Don't you agree, Charles?"

"Well, er . . ." The actor didn't feel up to pursuing this metaphor. He indicated the director's wine glass. "Get you another of those, Gavin?"

"Thanks."

7

Charles looked along the counter, but there was no sign of the barman. Everything was empty and unready, the Pinero Theatre gearing itself up slowly to the start of another season of creative endeavour.

"I think Norman's just putting on another beer barrel," said Gavin. "He'll be back in a min."

But the break in their conversation did not deflect him from his theorizing. "You see, Charles, I think this is the only way that Macbeth's behaviour makes any kind of sense. He's not a particularly sensitive man—indeed, he's probably the least sensitive of all Shakespeare's tragic heroes—so when he suddenly develops an imagination, the shock is profound. Cataclysmic almost. Don't you agree?"

Charles nodded and, as he did so, remembered that Gavin had always been like this, always seeking agreement to bolster his vulnerable confidence. He remembered, too, that Gavin had always been a talker, and that he always selected one person in every production as his confidant, the honoured recipient of long anxieties over many drinks at the end of each day's rehearsals. Charles was rather afraid that he had got that particular short straw, that he had been cast in the role for the duration of Gavin's production of *Macbeth*.

As the director continued to impose his preconceptions on Shakespeare, Charles thought back to how he had got the job, how elated he had been to hear about it, how conveniently his mind had forgotten what a bore Gavin Scholes in full flood could be.

The call had come through from Charles's agent, Maurice Skellern. One afternoon in early August, the actor had been lying on the yellow candlewick bedspread of his Hereford Road bedsitter, trying to remember what being in work felt like, when he had heard the payphone on the landing ring. Assuming it was yet another call connected with the bemusingly complicated sex-lives of the Amazonian Swedish girls who occupied most of the other bedsitters, he had let it ring on until it became

8

clear that he was alone in the house. Only then had he stirred himself to answer it.

"Charles, it's Maurice."

For his agent to ring him was sufficiently unusual for Charles to do a quick mental checklist of what the call could possibly be about. A cheque for a fee due on the sale to Zambia of some long-forgotten television series had just come in? No, Maurice would never ring him to mention that; the agent's method was to sit on any money that came in until he was virtually prised off his chair.

The National Theatre had finally seen the error of its ways and was inviting him to give his Lear? No, no, Charles, don't be ridiculous, you're far too old and cynical even to give such fantasies mind-room (and yet he still did, he still did).

No, to be realistic, if Maurice was calling him, it was bound to be something riveting like a National Insurance enquiry.

So, without much optimism, he had replied, "Hello, Maurice. What gives?"

"Charles, you know I've been saying for some time that you ought to be getting back to your roots, in the classical theatre . . . ?"

Charles didn't know this. So far as he could recall, Maurice had never said anything of the kind. On the rare occasions that the agent did proffer any advice on what the actor laughingly referred to as his career, the recommendation had always been, "Get a good telly, Charles. That's where the money is."

But there was never any point in taking issue with Maurice on minor points like the truth. Charles confined his response to a non-committal grunt.

"Well, I think," Maurice went on, "that my careful ground-work's beginning to pay off."

Again, Charles could not be bothered to contest this. Maurice was congenitally incapable of careful groundwork. If any offer of work had come in for one of his clients, it had nothing to do with the agent's ministrations. Any groundwork that had been done had been done by the client himself. Or the offer had just come in out of the blue.

So it proved. But Maurice once again demonstrated that, whatever his shortcomings in other aspects of an agent's work, he was highly skilled at taking for himself any credit that might be available.

"Listen, I've just had a call from Gavin Scholes . . ."

"Oh yes? He's Artistic Director of some place out in the West Country now, isn't he?"

"The Pinero Theatre, Warminster." There was a note of reproof in Maurice's voice, implying that the least his client could do was to keep up to date with who was in charge of the various provincial theatres. Since Charles was confident that his agent had been unaware of Gavin's appointment until the moment of his telephone call, this too was mildly galling.

"Anyway, he's just starting a new season, doing *Macbeth*, and, thanks to all the ringing round and prodding I've been doing . . ." (Lies, lies, thought Charles) ". . . he's specifically asked for you to join the company."

"Oh." Any offer of work was gratifying. And, once again, despite the curbs his cynicism tried to impose on them, Charles's fantasies strained at the end of their leashes. He'd worked with Gavin Scholes a couple of times, and the director had always seemed pleased with what he'd done. So it should be a substantial part. Banquo, maybe . . . ? That was all right, you got the nice haunting bit in the Banquet scene . . . unless you'd got one of those stupid directors who thought the ghost should be invisible. . . . Hmm, trouble with Banquo was, he did tend to fade away a bit in the second half. . . . Excellent part, though, for nipping off to the pub after the interval and just staggering back in time for the curtain call . . .

There are quite a few good Shakespearean parts like that, actually . . . Tybalt in *Romeo and Juliet*, that's terrific, killed off in Act Three Scene One. . . . The one you want to avoid at all costs is bloody Fortinbras in *Hamlet*. One boring scene leading your soldiers, then you have to wait right till the very end of the play for your "Go, bid the soldiers shoot" routine. . . . And *Hamlet*'s such a long play, it nearly always finishes after closing time, anyway . . .

Or what about Duncan in *Macbeth* . . . ? Charles wondered. He's certainly a good boozer's part . . . gets killed off good and early. . . . Trouble is, though, he hasn't got many lines, and directors have a nasty habit of doubling him with the Scottish Doctor in the Sleepwalking Scene, which really wreaks havoc with your drinking. . . . And, surely, Charles thought, I'm not old enough for Duncan, am I? I mean, that's a real old stager's part . . . not right for someone who's . . . well, let's say in their fifties . . .

Macduff, though . . . Not a bad part. True, he goes a bit quiet in the middle of the play, and he has got that turgid scene with Malcolm in England . . . But, on the other hand, he gets good chances of a bit of emoting when he hears his family's been killed . . . *And*, of course, he's got the swordfight at the end. Yes, quite a lot to be said for Macduff.

Or . . . was it possible . . . ? Charles had been around for a long time . . . He'd certainly got the experience for the role . . . And Gavin did like his work . . . Hadn't the director said, when Charles had been giving his Lane the Manservant in *The Importance of Being Earnest* ("subtly insolent"—*Yorkshire Post*), that he'd like to work with him in a bigger part . . . ? Yes, it was about time . . . After all, why not? Every director has to take a chance some time . . . And every actor has to get his big break some time . . . And, God knew, Charles had waited long enough.

Yes, why not Charles Paris as Macbeth?

All this flashed through his mind in actor's mental shorthand before he casually asked Maurice, "What's the part?"

"Well, he definitely wants you to do the Bleeding Sergeant in Act One."

"Ah," said Charles. Thirty-six lines, if his memory served him correctly. Mind you, thirty-six lines of fairly long-winded poetry . . . a lot of directors cut a few of them.

"And he wants you to double the Drunken Porter."

"Oh yes." Thirty-three lines. And that worst of all fates, a Shakespearean character who's meant to be funny. Charles was prepared to believe that lines like "Have napkins enow about you; here you'll sweat for it" got belters from the groundlings at the Globe; but he knew that to a modern audience they were about as funny as a rise in the mortgage rate.

"Still," Maurice went on, "Gavin says there could be other good parts in the offing."

"Oh." Well, that was encouraging. Maybe not in *Macbeth*, but there might be leads in later productions. "Is it a booking for the season?"

"Well, no, it's just *Macbeth* at the moment. Gavin's booking one production at a time . . . but he was optimistic that there could be some other good parts."

"And what money are they offering?"

Maurice told him.

Charles winced. "They've got to pay more than that. You're going to push for more, aren't you?"

"Oh, Charles . . ." Maurice sounded mortally offended. "What do you take me for?"

Charles restrained himself from answering that one.

"I'll be as tough as nails. Got to earn my fifteen per cent, haven't I?"

"Yes. Maurice, I'm still not happy about this fifteen per cent business. Most agents only take ten. I mean, I know you call it Personal Management, but I haven't really seen much evidence that—"

"Charles, trust me."

"Hmm."

"I'll screw them for every penny they've got. And then a few. Come on, Charles, you know me, don't you?"

"Yes," Charles agreed gloomily.

He knew the sort of money he would get. Maurice might screw another five a week out of them, but it was still going to be an income most tea-ladies would reject with derision. A lot of actors, he knew, just said they couldn't afford to do rep. "Love to do it, darling, super part, and I really want to get back to my roots in the live theatre, but I'm afraid, with the money they were offering, the sums just don't add up."

But the people who said that were actors who had good chances of getting parts in television. The sums didn't add up for Charles either, but in his case there weren't at that moment any other options.

And even the pittance that the Pinero Theatre, Warminster, was offering was more than the dole. Just.

And it was work. He felt ridiculously elated when he put the phone down. Like most actors, he went into a sort of limbo, a suspended animation, when he wasn't working. Now at least he had a chance to do what he was supposed to do.

And the parts weren't really that bad. Already he was starting to think of the accents he would use for the two. Something contrasting. Yes, be nice to get a notice like he had when playing Pompey and the Clown in *Antony and Cleopatra* ("an acutely differentiated pair of cameos by Charles Paris"—*Western Evening News*).

Hmm, the Bleeding Sergeant and the Drunken Porter . . . Not at all bad.

And it could have been a lot worse. Charles recalled the opening stage direction for *Macbeth* Act One Scene Seven: "Enter a Sewer."

At least he hadn't got that part.

"Now the question is, of course, how much imagination has Lady Macbeth got? That's the important thing, isn't it, Charles?"

"Er, sorry?" With an effort he dragged his concentration back to what Gavin was saying. "Yes, yes," he said, opting for a safe response.

"She's obviously not such a stranger to the imaginative dimension as Macbeth himself is. Is she?"

"No," Charles agreed, continuing his safety play. So long as he got the Yesses, Noes and Ahs in the right places, he reckoned he'd be all right.

"I mean, clearly, when we first see her, reading Macbeth's letter, she has already imagined the possibility of her husband becoming King. Wouldn't you agree?"

"Oh yes." He added the "Oh" for simple variety.

"But just *how* imaginative is she? I mean, could Lady Macbeth cope with the Weird Sisters?"

"Ah . . ."

"And indeed does she get less imaginative as Macbeth gets more imaginative? Does she actually—?"

The US Cavalry, in the form of the barman, appeared at the end of the counter and Charles, whose ammunition against death by boredom was running dangerously low, hailed the lifesaver effusively.

"Could we have the same again, please?"

"Sure." The barman took their glasses. He was a quiet man, whose face was permanently set in an expression of rueful apology.

While their drinks were being served, Charles made a determined effort to shift the conversation away from Gavin Scholes' theory of hidden resonances in Shakespeare's text. There'd be time enough for all that once they started actual rehearsal. It was the Saturday evening; they'd got till Monday morning before they had to address themselves to the problems of interpretation and characterization. And Charles didn't really think that finding the concealed behavioural triggers of the Bleeding Sergeant and the Drunken Porter was going to take him that long.

"Who else is in the company, Gavin?"

"Well, I told you George Birkitt is giving his Macbeth . . . You ever worked with him, Charles?"

"Yes." Charles left it at that. No point in going into the details of his previous encounters with George, on a television sit com called *The Strutters*, in a play called *The Hooded Owl* which had transferred to the West End, most recently on the

14

pilot of a ghastly television game-show entitled *If The Cap Fits*. Nor did Charles wish to be drawn on what he thought of George Birkitt's talent as an actor.

"Very lucky to get him," said Gavin. "Big telly name like that."

"Yes."

"He's got to have a couple of rehearsal days out for filming some new sit com he's doing, but basically we've got him right through."

"Oh, good," said Charles, permitting himself an edge of irony. Down at his level in the profession, you didn't get days off rehearsal for doing other jobs; it was only so-called stars who could get that kind of thing written into their contracts.

But Gavin seemed unaware of the intonation. "Then I was terribly lucky to get Felicia Chatterton for Lady Macbeth. Ever come across her?"

Charles shook his head.

"No, well, you wouldn't have done unless you'd been with the Royal Shakespeare. She went straight out of Central to Stratford and hasn't worked anywhere else. Done some lovely stuff . . . super notices for her Perdita. And a smashing Celia. Anyway, like most of them do, she's now venturing out into the real commercial world."

"How old is she?"

"Late twenties."

"Bit young to be partnered by George, isn't she?"

"Oh, I don't know. She's very clever. And, anyway, I think a younger Lady Macbeth helps the sensuality in the relationship. Don't you?"

Charles tried another nod this time.

"The sexual dimension is so important. You know, that whole business of whether she's had children or not. . . . She has the 'I have given suck . . .' speech, but then Macduff says, 'He has no children.' Now, are we meant to assume—?"

"Yes." Charles diverted the subject forcibly. "Who else is there?"

"What, in the company?"

"Yes. Who's Duncan, for instance?"

"Oh." Gavin smiled slyly. "I got Warnock Belvedere for that."

"Ah."

"From your tone of voice, I gather you know him."

"Only by reputation."

Again Gavin Scholes read something in Charles's intonation. "Oh, I think that's probably all bullshit. I mean, you know how easily someone gets a name for being difficult. One director they don't get on with, and suddenly all these stories start circulating round the business. I'm sure he'll be fine."

"You haven't worked with him?"

"No. I've spoken to him on the phone, and he sounds absolutely charming. Anyway, when you book someone like that, one of those larger-than-life characters, in my experience you get so much in return. You know, those older actors really know how to fill the stage. Don't you agree?"

Charles did agree, and said "Yes." But he didn't say that, in his experience, actors who "filled the stage" hadn't a lot of time for the other actors who tried to share it with them.

"Oh, I'm not worried," Gavin went on breezily, though something in his expression belied the words. "With most so-called difficult actors, I think it's all down to how the director handles them. Don't you agree?"

This time there was no mistaking the naked appeal in Gavin's eyes. It confirmed Charles's suspicion that he had been booked as much to give the director moral support as to give his Bleeding Sergeant and Drunken Porter.

"No, there'll be no problem," Gavin continued protesting too much. "Most actors who behave badly are just insecure. If you take a firm line from the start—"

But the director didn't get time to articulate his full theory of how to deal with difficult actors. Behind them the swing doors into the bar clattered dramatically open and a huge fruity voice boomed out, "Who do you have to fuck to get a drink round here?"

Gavin Scholes and Charles Paris looked round. But they both knew what they would see before they saw it.

A mountainous man propped up on a silver-topped walking stick swayed near the door. He wore a shapeless suit of thick checked tweed over a bottle-green waistcoat across which a watch-chain hung pretentiously. His mane of white hair and beard seemed to have been modelled on the elderly Buffalo Bill. A monocle was screwed firmly into the veined purple face.

"Charles Paris," said Gavin Scholes as he moved towards the door, "I don't believe you've met Warnock Belvedere . . . ?"

Chapter Two

THE OLD ACTOR'S presence was so commanding that it was only as Gavin and Charles drew near that they noticed he had not entered the bar alone. Slightly behind Warnock, eclipsed by his bulk, stood a thin boy, scarcely out of his teens, on whose face an eager-to-please smile hovered nervously.

"Oh, hello, Russ. Charles, I don't think you've met Russ Lavery either . . . ?"

"No, I—"

"Never mind that," boomed Warnock Belvedere. "Time enough for pleasantries when you've got me that bloody drink. God, a man could die of dehydration in this place."

"Yes, yes, of course," said Gavin, scuttling back to the bar, and suggesting to Charles that the director's "firm line" in dealing with the supposedly difficult actor would be based on abject subservience.

"What's it to be?" Gavin asked from the bar.

"Brandy. Large one," Warnock Belvedere replied as he limped heavily across the room.

Charles reached out his hand to the young man who had been introduced as Russ Lavery. "Charles Paris. Are you in the company?"

"Yes, it's my first job out of Webber Douglas."

"Welcome to the business."

"Thanks. Yes, I just finished my training this summer. I was very lucky. An agent liked what I did in one of the final term productions and signed me up."

"Well done."

"It was Robbie Patrick, actually."

The boy was demonstrably keen to get the name into the

18

conversation. And with reason. Robbie Patrick was one of the most successful and fashionable agents on the scene. To be signed up by him was about the best start any aspiring actor could have.

"Anyway, Robbie put me up to audition for Gavin and it went okay, and I've got one of the Pinero's provisional cards."

"Again, well done." It was quite an achievement. The actors' union, Equity, paranoid about too many people entering a hopelessly overcrowded profession, restricted most theatres to admitting two new members a year. To have got one of the coveted union cards so quickly was what every drama student in the country prayed for.

"What are you playing?" asked Charles, with a grin.

The grin had the right effect, and the boy seemed more relaxed as he replied, "Fleance and Young Siward."

"Great."

"Yes, I'm very excited about it. You know, the chance to play two contrasting roles. Using different voices."

There was something puppyish about the boy's enthusiasm. Charles for a moment felt almost patronizing, until he reflected that he himself had reacted in exactly the same way to the prospect of playing two minor roles.

"I'm sure you'll have lots of fun," he said.

"Yes, I mean just the chance to work in a company with—"

"Come over here, boy!" Warnock Belvedere bellowed from the bar. "Come and sit by me. Pretty boy's just bought me dinner. Least I can do is to get him a drink."

Russ Lavery flushed and moved across to the bar. Charles followed more slowly. He didn't like the sound of what Warnock had just said. The old actor was a notorious sponger, but to sponge off someone like Russ seemed pretty shabby. Nearly all actors are poor, but the ones who've just finished drama school tend to be even poorer than the rest.

Nor did Charles like the "pretty boy" reference. Warnock Belvedere's reputation encompassed fairly aggressive homosexuality, and Charles hoped that Russ wasn't going to find himself in an awkward situation with the old actor. There was an air of naïveté about the youngster, which was capable of misinterpreting Warnock's interest as something more altruistic, the simple desire of an old stager to help someone making his first tentative steps in the business.

Charles's misgivings were not dispelled when the old actor put his arm round the young one's shoulders and hoisted him on to a barstool. "Now what's it to be, Russ? It's still Gavin's round, so ask for whatever you want."

Russ Lavery coloured. "Oh, after all that wine we had at dinner, I don't think I need anything else—"

"'O! reason not the need!'" Warnock quoted grandiloquently, prompting Charles to wonder whether the old actor had ever actually played Lear. If he ever did, Charles thought vindictively, I bet it was a really hammy Lear.

"Good heavens," Warnock continued, "you can't come into this business if you can't take your liquor. Christ, boy, what do you think keeps the theatre going? It's not talent, it's not arty-farty acting, it's not bloody Arts Council grants—it's alcohol, pure and simple. Wouldn't you agree?"

This last was flashed maliciously at Charles, who found the question a slightly uncomfortable one to answer. Much as he hated to side with Warnock Belvedere, he could not deny the considerable contribution that alcohol (in particular, Bell's whisky) had made to his own theatrical career.

"Come on, boy, have something."

"Well, um, a small sherry."

"Sherry! After dinner. Good God, have you just let go Mummy's apron-strings? Don't you know anything?"

Russ Lavery looked deeply humiliated. It was clear that the answer to both Warnock's questions was affirmative. Charles observed how, as with the snipe at him about alcohol, the old actor had a knack of homing in on people's private anxieties. It made him a potentially difficult person to deal with.

"Get the boy a sherry," Warnock ordered, and Gavin Scholes obediently reached for his wallet.

"Sweet, medium or dry?" Norman the barman asked impassively.

The old actor looked at Russ. "Well, come on boy. You must give Mine Host an answer. I'm afraid I don't know the appropriate etiquette for after-dinner sherry drinking."

The boy blushed as his humiliation was rubbed in. "Dry, please," he said in a small voice.

Still impassive, Norman poured the drink. Warnock, seeming for a moment to regret his cruelty, continued in a softer voice. "Oh, I remember, when I was young, I once made a terrible cock-up over drink. It was when I was working with Ralph . . ."

"Ralph Richardson?" asked Russ Lavery, awestruck.

"Yes," Warnock Belvedere conceded casually, well aware of the impact his words were having. "I was quite new to the business . . . maybe a little older than you—and not nearly as pretty, I'm afraid . . ."

Russ looked confused, confirming Charles's suspicion that the boy didn't know how to deal with this homosexual badinage. It's always difficult in the theatre. There's so much effusiveness, so much jokey campness that it's sometimes hard to spot an authentically gay approach. In this case, though, Charles could have told Russ that he was up against the real thing.

"Anyway, at the end of the rehearsal one day, Ralph said he'd buy us all a drink. I was about as clueless as you are, young Russ, so I thought, well, here we are in the big, glamorous theatrical world, and I asked him for a glass of champagne. Hadn't a clue what it cost. And in those days, it was going to be a question of opening a bottle—none of this wine-bar nonsense where they keep one open under the counter. Anyway, give the old darling his due, he bought it for me without demur. Handed me the glass, and, as he did so, he said—very straight-faced, 'You show good taste, young man. If you always insist on living life by champagne standards, there's no reason why you shouldn't succeed. No one ever lost out by aiming too high.

"Ah, but a man's reach should exceed his grasp,
Or what's a heaven for?"'
Never forgotten that bit of advice, you know."

Needless to say, for the reported lines, the old actor dropped into impersonation. Charles had yet to encounter an actor who didn't do an impression of the late Sir Ralph Richardson. The quality varied from reasonable verisimilitude to a kind of decrepit bleat, but every actor had one tucked away for the vast supply of stories, true and apocryphal, which had accreted round that larger-than-life figure.

Warnock Belvedere's impersonation was actually rather good, but whether or not Richardson had ever given him the advice claimed or had ever quoted Browning at him, Charles doubted.

Russ Lavery was, however, impressed and so Warnock Belvedere pressed home his advantage with one of the more familiar Richardson anecdotes.

"Actually, dear old Ralph . . ." (He pronounced it "Rafe", needless to say) ". . . once did something rather wonderful at a first night of some turgid new play he was doing. Started the First Act and, you know, they were getting nothing from the audience, but nothing. Obviously the thing was a real turkey . . . flopperoonie wasn't in it. . . . So suddenly Ralph stops in the middle of a speech, walks down to the footlights, and says to the audience, 'Is there a doctor in the house?'

"Little bloke stands up at the back of the stalls. 'Yes, I'm a doctor.'

"'Doctor,' says Ralph, 'isn't this a terrible play?'"

Though familiar to Charles, the story was well told, and he joined in the laughter that greeted its punchline. Even the barman Norman allowed himself a flicker of a smile. But, as Charles laughed, he wondered why Warnock Belvedere had suddenly turned so affable. He had a nasty feeling that the old actor wanted to ingratiate himself back into favour with Russ Lavery; he realized he'd pushed too far about the sherry, and was now making up for that lapse. What Warnock's ulterior motive was, Charles didn't think would be too difficult to guess.

Before the old actor could plunge into another anecdote of the distinguished company he kept, the bar-room doors rattled again and they all turned to look at the new arrival.

It was a woman, mid to late forties. Her hair was probably naturally black, but had been assisted to a uniform blackness which did not quite look natural. The blue eyes were rimmed with heavy make-up and her slightly sulky mouth was outlined in a harsh red. She wore a tight black skirt, seamed black stockings and shiny cream blouse. Chunky jewellery clustered at her neck and on her wrists. She didn't quite look tarty, but damn nearly.

Gavin and Norman's reactions to the arrival showed that she was a familiar figure in the theatre. The barman seemed to look away with disinterest, while the director gave a little wave and called out, "Sandra, love. Get you a drink?"

"Please. A Tia Maria."

Norman had the bottle in his hand and was pouring from it before she said the words.

"Oh, I've just finished sorting it all out," the woman sighed, depositing herself with elaborate mock-exhaustion on the bar-stool.

"The postal bookings?" asked Gavin.

She nodded. "Using credit cards is supposed to make the whole thing simpler, and I'm sure it does when everyone gets their details right. But when they ask for the wrong price, or the wrong night . . . huh. Some of them even get their credit card numbers wrong."

Gavin moved the glass of dark brown fluid across the bar to her. "Never mind, you'll feel better after this."

"Thanks." She took a long, grateful swallow.

"Sorry, should introduce you. Warnock Belvedere . . . Charles Paris . . . Russ Lavery . . ." The actors nodded acknowledgement. "This is a most essential lady—our Box Office Manager—or should it be Manageress . . . ?"

"Manager. I do the job quite as well as a man would," she insisted with perhaps unnecessary vehemence.

"You certainly do," Gavin Scholes gave a sycophantic smile of agreement. "Sandra Phipps."

She smiled round at them, then said, "Give us a packet of peanuts, Norman. I'm starving."

The barman handed them over, asking for, and apparently expecting, no money in return.

Sandra glared at him. "Don't look so hangdog. We will get something to eat later."

"I didn't say anything."

"No, you just looked it. We'll pick up a Chinkie on the way home."

"Fine." The barman turned to straighten up the rows of fruit juice bottles.

Gavin Scholes stepped into the rather awkward silence that ensued. "Should explain, Sandra and Norman are married."

"Oy," she said skittishly. "Don't spoil my chances with all these lovely young actors."

"Thank you for the 'young', Madam." Warnock Belvedere leant across and kissed her hand with mock-courtesy. "Nicest thing anyone's said to me all evening." Then, in an elaborate aside, he whispered, "Fancy nipping down the car park for a quickie?"

Knowing the actor's sexual orientation, Charles found this remark unbearably arch, but it appealed to Sandra Phipps, who burst into a raucous ripple of giggles.

"All the same, you bloody men," she accused (inaccurately, as it happened, in Warnock's case), "only think about one thing." Then, with a glance at Norman's back, added, "With exceptions, of course."

Clearly, this sexual sniping was part of the couple's relationship. It made Charles feel rather uncomfortable.

Gavin again stepped in as the peacemaker. "I tell you, without Sandra and Norman, the Pinero would just literally fall apart. I mean, sod the actors and directors, if you don't sell the tickets, you're left with a marked lack of bums on seats. And, if the audience can't get a drink in the interval, well, it's the end of everything."

"And, if the cast can't," said Warnock, banging his glass on the counter to attract Norman's attention, "it's the end of civilization as we know it."

Silently, the barman refilled the brandy glass and looked around quizzically at the others. Russ Lavery shook his head, but the rest signalled acquiescence and had their glasses recharged.

"How's the advance?" Charles asked Sandra Phipps, feeling he should show an interest in her work.

"Pretty good. Considering we don't open for nearly a month. Fridays and Saturdays okay—though a lot of those are subscription seats—and the Schools' Matinees are virtually full."

"Comes of doing a set text," said Gavin smugly. "All the kids have to come and see it or they're going to make a balls-up of their exams. Eminently satisfactory."

"For the management, maybe," said Charles. "Not so hot for the actors."

"What do you mean?" asked Warnock Belvedere.

"Well, maybe you've been lucky enough not to have had to do any Schools' Matinees, but—"

This was clearly the wrong thing to say. Warnock bridled. "I'll have you know, I have performed in every kind of theatre that there is. I've done more bloody Schools' Matinees than you've had hot dinners."

"All right. Sorry. But then you know what I'm talking about."

"No."

"I mean the kids' behaviour. None of them are there because they want to be. It's just a chore. Another boring old lesson —except with the advantage that the lights are out. As a result, they do all the things they'd like to do at school. If they're single sex schools, they fight and giggle. If they're mixed, you've pretty soon got a full-scale orgy."

"That has not been my experience," said Warnock loftily. "I find that that sort of thing only happens when they've got nothing interesting to look at on stage. When they're looking at actors of stature . . . when they're seeing people who can properly *command* a stage, the problem does not arise."

The inference was there—and it was a fairly insulting one —but Charles could not be bothered to pick it up. Warnock Belvedere was one of those people who thrives on reaction to their rudeness. Give them nothing back, and their attack is disarmed.

So it proved. After a few seconds of staring at Charles, the old actor gave up and turned pointedly towards Russ Lavery. "Actually, dear boy, there's another story about Ralph I must tell you. It's a weeny bit smutty, but I'm sure you don't mind a bit of smut . . ."

At the same moment Gavin left, saying he just had to check something in the office, so Charles had to make conversation with Sandra Phipps. Under normal circumstances, this would not have been a chore. She was attractive enough, and could chatter along quite merrily at a level of harmless but covert innuendo.

However, with her husband so close, Charles felt a little awkward. Particularly as she was obviously keeping up the innuendo principally for Norman's benefit. Charles wasn't interested in how they brought excitement into their marriage. That was up to them. But he just wished they wouldn't involve him.

Sandra started in the way she intended to continue. "So you know I'm married—in name, anyway—how about you? You tied up or are you available?"

"Well . . ." said Charles, very conscious of Norman's proximity.

"Go on, don't be coy. Are you married?"

"Yes. Technically."

"What on earth does that mean?"

26

Charles wished he knew. He and Frances were not divorced, but he would have been hard put to define exactly how close their relationship was. At times, although they lived apart, it could still be very close. But this wasn't one of those times. In fact, they were probably further apart at that moment than they had been at any stage in their lives.

It was his fault. As usual. But admitting that didn't make it any easier to accept. Basically, he had blown it. He had stood Frances up. He had invited her out to dinner, then he had got delayed and when he arrived at the restaurant, there had been no sign of her.

All right, that wasn't such a big deal. That sort of thing had happened many times in the course of their switchback relationship. What was different this time was the way Frances had reacted to the affront. When they'd made the dinner arrangement, she'd instructed him to be there on time "or forget it". But then she'd often said things like that. What made this time different was that she clearly meant it.

She actually wouldn't speak to him on the phone. As soon as she recognized the voice, down went the receiver. Being an actor, of course, he could sometimes make it difficult for her *to* recognize his voice, but once he had engaged her in conversation in the spurious guise of a Glaswegian plumber or an Indian double-glazing salesman, there had to come the moment when he changed back to himself and tried to say what he wanted to. And each time he got to that point, she put the phone down.

Only once had she spoken directly to him since the broken dinner date. And her words then had been among the most hurtful he had ever heard.

"You're not good for me, Charles Paris."

That was all she had said. Then, once again, the receiver had gone down.

Of course, he could have tried to go and see her. Arrive on the doorstep of her flat in Highgate, waylay her as she set out for the school of which she was headmistress. But always something stopped him. Basic inertia. The sudden need to have a drink, to go out and meet people, other actors, people he wasn't *close* to.

And maybe, after all, Frances was right. Maybe he was bad for her. Maybe they were better off apart. After all, he was the one who had walked out all those years before, walked out in the search of a freedom which he knew, even as he left, would prove illusory.

And, since Frances had made no attempt to make contact, perhaps she was better off with him erased from the map of her life.

He only wished he felt the same.

And now here he was, working miles away from her, and she probably didn't even know he was in Warminster. Somehow, he must re-establish contact. Send her a card, perhaps . . . ? He'd have to have something to say on it, though . . .

"Come on, it wasn't that difficult a question. Not as if I'd asked you if you could remember how many times you done it or something like that."

Sandra Phipps' words, and the suggestive giggle that followed them, brought him back to the Pinero Theatre, Warminster.

"Sorry, miles away."

"You can say that again. Naughty fantasies, I dare say."

"No, not in fact. I . . ." It didn't seem worth continuing. "Have you been working here in the theatre long?" he asked, moving to a dull, uncontroversial subject that should offer few opportunities for double meanings.

"Getting on for fifteen years in all."

"Really?" said Charles, sounding impressed, because she had said it in a way that demanded an impressed reaction.

"Yes. Well, there was a break in the middle when I went off to have my baby."

"Ah."

"Stewart. He's thirteen now." She smoothed down her

blouse over her waist. "Do I really look old enough to have a great big son aged thirteen?"

Again, Charles gave the expected reaction, though in fact Stewart's age was no surprise to him. He wouldn't have fallen off his bar-stool if she'd said she had a son of twenty-five.

"Actually, you'll be seeing Stewart soon."

"Oh, will I?" Charles was all in favour of keeping the conversation going about her son; it seemed to be the only subject which she didn't infuse with double meanings.

"Stewart's in the play."

"In *Macbeth*?"

"Yes. He's playing Macduff's son."

"That must be very exciting for you."

"Ooh, and for him. He's really chuffed. Has to get licensed and everything."

"Of course."

"And he'll have to have some time off school. But, touch wood, they're being very good about it. Say it's fine, so long as his work doesn't suffer. But Stewart's a bright boy . . . not really academic, but bright."

"Oh, good. So we'll see him at the readthrough on Monday?"

"Well, no. School wants him to be off the minimum time, so he'll be coming for the first time when Gavin's blocking his scenes. Thursday afternoon, it should be."

"I look forward to meeting him. Maybe the start of a great theatrical career." Charles provided the platitudes automatically.

"We'll see. Maybe the start of a great career of me as a theatrical Mum." Sandra let out an appalled giggle at the prospect. "Aren't they the ones who have to sleep with all the producers . . . ?"

"No, I don't think so," said Charles evenly, trying to crush that particular conversational opening at source.

"Last orders," said Norman lugubriously.

"Is it really?" Charles looked at his watch. Yes, it was. "How time flies when you're inebriating yourself. Look, this is my round."

Another Tia Maria for Sandra. Large brandy for Warnock. Assume Gavin would want another large white wine. "Russ . . . ?"

"No. No, I really must go back to my digs."

"Oh, come on, dear boy. It's not that late," Warnock protested.

"Sorry. Really must go."

Abruptly the young man left the bar. The abruptness suggested either that he was going to be sick from the unaccustomed alcohol, or that Warnock had made some unequivocal suggestion to him that he didn't like. The expression of frustrated annoyance on Warnock Belvedere's face made Charles favour the second interpretation.

"Bloody kids!" the old actor grumbled. "Hardly out of nappies and they're trying to get on to the stage. Huh." Then, in a cruelly accurate parody of Russ's earnestly breathless voice, he parroted, "'I played Richard II at Webber Douglas. The local paper gave me a smashing notice. And I've got this wonderful agent, Robbie Patrick.' Huh. What the hell does he think he knows about theatre?"

"Time," said Norman quietly.

Warnock Belvedere drained his brandy glass in one and slammed it down on the table. "Right, Mine Host, give me another one."

"I'm sorry. I just called 'time'."

"I don't give a wet fart what you called. I asked for another brandy."

"I'm sorry, Mr Belvedere. I can't serve you. I am the licensee of this bar, and I'm afraid I can't risk trouble with the police."

"Oh, come on, for Christ's sake!" Elaborately, Warnock looked around the empty bar. "Look at all the police. Place is bloody swarming with them, isn't it? Don't be so pathetic. Give me a drink."

"I'm sorry."

"Norman, don't be so bloody pussy-footed!" Disloyally, but predictably, Sandra Phipps joined the attack.

"I've told you. I can't."

"Give me a bloody drink!" This time Warnock slammed his glass down with such force that it broke.

"I'm afraid I'll have to charge you for that glass," said Norman Phipps evenly.

"No, you bloody won't! You're not going to charge me for anything! Do you know who I am? I'm not just anyone, you know. I'm not some little teenage shit just out of drama school. I am Warnock Belvedere, and when I bloody ask you for a drink, I bloody get one!"

The barman shook his head. "No."

Warnock's voice had reached fever pitch. "Look, am I going to have to—?"

He stopped at the sound of the bar doors, which heralded Gavin's return.

"Any trouble?" asked the director, with a coolness belied by the nervous glint in his eyes.

"Mr Belvedere wants a drink and I've called time."

"Ah. . . . Ah." Gavin Scholes for a moment looked as if he might make a stand, but quickly caved in. "Give him a drink, Norman."

"But I can't—"

"I'll take the responsibility."

"That's all very well, but it's not your responsibility. I am the licensee and—"

"Oh, shut up and give him the bloody drink, Norman," snapped Sandra.

Wordlessly, Norman took a clean brandy balloon from the shelf and filled it with a large measure. He placed it in front of Warnock Belvedere, then picked up a small dustpan and brush, and cleared the debris of the other glass.

"Thank you. About bloody time, too." The old actor raised the glass in the air. "Cheers," he said. "Here's to the Scottish Play."

He downed the drink in one. No one spoke as he moved to the bar-room door. He stopped and looked back ruminatively, as if selecting an appropriate exit line.

"The Scottish Play," he repeated. "Yes, The Caledonian Tragedy . . . The Harry Lauder Show . . . call it what you like, it really is bad luck, you know. Not just superstition. Something always goes wrong with a production of the Scottish Play. Accident . . . illness . . . death . . . murder even." He laughed abruptly and triumphantly. "I wonder which it's going to be this time . . . ?"

He turned on his heel, surprisingly agile for a man who walked always with a stick, and pushed through the doors.

They clattered closed behind him, unnaturally loud in the vacuum of silence he had left.

Chapter Three

FIRST READTHROUGHS ARE always edgy occasions and the Monday morning one for *Macbeth* at the Pinero Theatre, Warminster, was no exception.

The edginess arises from insecurity. Everyone present is worried about the first impression they are creating. The director and resident staff of the theatre are in the position of hosts, anxious that their guests will be happy with the facilities offered. Some of the cast may be concerned about their parts and how they're going to play them, some still raw from their agents' unsuccessful battles to screw more money out of the administration. And all of the company are wary, stalking round each other, antennae acutely adjusted to get the feel of the people they will be working with for the next few weeks. In the theatre there are happy companies and unhappy companies. Every actor knows how miserable it is to spend a couple of months in an unhappy company, so at the first readthrough they are all trying to gauge the feeling of the ensemble.

And whereas dogs express this kind of anxiety by sniffing at potential invaders, in actors the unease is translated into a kind of flamboyant jokiness. Voices are too loud, only moderately amusing anecdotes are greeted with excessive laughter, and a lot of extravagant hugging goes on.

In most companies everyone will already know someone, or at least have mutual friends. These relationships are quickly re-established, and so before the readthrough starts, the actors and actresses form into little clusters of badinage. Even Russ Lavery, new to the business, by having come down to Warminster a few days before rehearsals started, had made enough contacts to have someone to talk to, as the terrifying moment of his first work as a professional actor began.

Charles Paris also had the advantage of having been there a few days, though, on reflection, he felt slightly resentful about that. Gavin had specifically requested that he come early "so that we can have a few jars and *really talk* before we all get swept up in rehearsal", but Charles was increasingly sure that the director had only suggested it because he needed moral support. Certainly, there had been no opportunity to *"really talk"*, and Charles felt he had been drafted in only as a buffer between Gavin and the potentially difficult Warnock Belvedere.

Still, he didn't feel that much resentment. His digs were comfortable, and he'd spent a peaceful Sunday exploring the pubs of Warminster, dozing with the papers between opening times and putting off further attempts to make contact with Frances.

So he felt remarkably cheerful on the Monday morning. He wasn't as tense as the rest of the company, many of whom had only driven down from London that morning. And, attractive though the double roles of Bleeding Sergeant and Drunken Porter were, he didn't actually feel too much anxiety about how he was going to play them. Home in on an accent, do the moves that Gavin gave him, and count a good performance as one in which he managed to wring a single laugh out of the Porter's dismally unfunny lines—that was how he intended to approach the job.

He was also delighted to see an unexpected, but welcomely familiar face at the readthrough. It was a snub-nosed, freckled face, belonging to John B. Murgatroyd, an actor with whom Charles had worked on numerous occasions and whose career was almost exactly as successful as his own (i.e. not very).

John B., they quickly established, would also be offering a double of amazing versatility to the good burghers of Warminster. He was to give his Lennox and First Murderer. "Not one of the most memorable Shakespearean roles, Lennox," he admitted to Charles, "but one I feel could be *profoundly rewarding.*" He slipped into a parody of thespian intensity. "I feel that the part is really only as good as the actor, and I'm sure, given the right performance, Lennox could become a *deeply significant role.*"

"Yes." Charles joined in the game, also adopting a manner of humourless earnestness. "Rather like the Bleeding Sergeant in that respect."

"Absolutely." John B. nodded sagely.

"And, as for the First Murderer . . ."

"One of the great Shakespearean roles."

"Exactly."

"So much depth. So much poetry."

"Oh yes."

"Do you know, Charles love . . ." The mocking intensity was becoming greater with each word ". . . when Gavin rang me about the production, he said, 'Look, old darling, I'll put my cards on the table. I'm doing *Macbeth* and I really want you to play the title role. But I know how you feel about the First Murderer, and if that's really what you decide, I'll have to bow to your decision. So what's it to be, old darling—Macbeth or First Murderer?' Well, of course, Charles, there was just no contest. I said to him straight away, 'Sorry, love, you'll have to find some inferior telly starlet for Macbeth. I'm not going to throw up the chance of First Murderer for anything.'"

The fantasy spluttered to an end in laughter. Charles felt encouraged. With John B. around, there was no danger that the next few weeks would be dull.

He looked across to the "inferior telly starlet" referred to. He had waved to George Birkitt when he first saw him but now the star of *What'll The Neighbours Say*, the ill-fated *Strutters* and other sit coms too humorous to mention, was sitting in the front row of the auditorium, the centre of a little cluster of sycophants.

Charles, who had watched George Birkitt's growth to fame, observed how the actor's face had become permanently set in the expression of someone opening a church bazaar or a supermarket. But there was now a nobler, more serious wrinkle to the brow. This, after all, was a significant moment, the actor who had found success in the mushroom medium of television, returning to his roots, demonstrating the more profound aspect of his character, the versatility which now made him ready to tackle one of the classic Shakespearean roles.

Charles tried to curb the uncharitable thoughts that the sight of George Birkitt always prompted. He knew that to think the actor's success was the product of a very moderate talent and a great deal of luck was probably only a sour grapes reaction.

And yet, he could never quite believe in George. He had watched the man who was about to give his Macbeth gradually gather the trappings of stardom, but he could never see the inward spark of genius that should irradiate a star. To Charles Paris, George Birkitt remained a perfectly amiable but rather dull actor, who had had a few lucky breaks and who was now too famous for anyone actually to observe that he wasn't particularly talented. Certainly, Charles allowed himself the bitchy thought, if Gavin Scholes saw Macbeth as a man devoid of imagination, it had been type-casting.

The other figure who had gathered a little coterie around him was, it went without saying, Warnock Belvedere. Like most self-appointed "characters", the old actor's reputation preceded him, and there was no one in the company who had not heard of him and was intrigued to meet the reality. There was a tendency in the theatre, which Charles disliked, for perfectly repellent people to be tolerated—and even lionized—simply on the basis of being "a character". Warnock fitted this role with relish, and was determined very deliberately to live up to his image. As Charles looked at him, he could hear the old actor once more name-dropping and pontificating. "Well, of course, I knew Larry back in the days when he was still with Vivien. Goodness, the two of them together were . . ."

Russ Lavery, Charles noticed with interest, was not in Warnock's circle of sycophants. He had joined the group around George Birkitt, exchanging the anecdotage of classical theatre for that of television Light Entertainment.

Only one member of the company sat alone, on an aisle seat halfway up the auditorium. She was strikingly pretty, small, with wispy blond hair scraped back into an artless knot. She wore a grey and purple designer jogging suit of the kind marketed to housewives who pretend to do aerobics. She was reading studiously, and the book was a copy of *Macbeth*.

By a process of elimination, Charles concluded that this must be the recent darling of the Royal Shakespeare Company, Felicia Chatterton, taking her first tentative step out of the womb of subsidized theatre into what Charles Paris thought of as the real world.

She looked intense, rather than tense. And she appeared to be reading the script, not as a pretence of having something to do, but because it interested her deeply.

Gavin Scholes appeared on stage and clapped his hands. The flamboyant chatter subsided raggedly, and over its end Warnock Belvedere's voice, in a well-judged stage whisper, was heard to say, "Oh Christ, it's that prat of a director."

Gavin joined in the little ripple of laughter which greeted this, but it clearly didn't make him any less nervous. He started in a voice of exaggerated bonhomie.

"Erm . . . yes, here I am, the prat of a director himself. Ha. First, I'd like to welcome you all to the Pinero Theatre, Warminster, for the first production of a new season, which is always exciting for all of us who work here. And also, it being the first production has a great practical advantage—namely, that we can rehearse from Day One on the stage, so we don't have all those hassles of suddenly discovering that the dimensions of the set as laid out in the rehearsal room are totally different from what we're faced with in the theatre. And let me tell you, with only three and a half weeks' rehearsal, we need all the advantages we can get!"

"Three and a half weeks?" echoed a thrillingly husky voice from the auditorium.

"Yes."

"But you can't do a Shakespeare in three and a half weeks . . ."

"Of course you can," said Gavin cheerfully. "I once put on *The Merchant* in ten days."

"Oh." From her tone, Felicia Chatterton did not seem to find this a very admirable achievement.

"But surely, Felicia love, your agent told you the schedule . . . ?"

"Well, yes he did," she admitted, "but I didn't believe him."

"Oh, well, he got it right. Three and a half weeks. Don't worry, it's going to be a great production," Gavin Scholes asserted with emphatic but diminishing confidence. "Now, I'd like to introduce our Company Manager, who's going to tell you a few things about how we run the Pinero . . ."

The Company Manager was like all Company Managers, and his spiel was the same as that of all Company Managers—details of the allocation of dressing rooms, places to eat (inside the theatre and out), where his office was, when those whose money didn't go directly to their agents would get paid, etc., etc., etc.

Charles switched off. He'd heard it many times before. But he was amused to see that Russ Lavery was drinking in every word. For the boy, just being there was magical, the consummation of all his dreams. He was a professional actor, embarking on his first professional job. The enthusiasm was almost embarrassing in its intensity.

Cynically, Charles Paris tried to remember if he had been so raw and callow when he had been in the same position at the end of the forties. Rather sheepishly, he concluded that he had been. Exactly the same, ecstatic with excitement just at the prospect of being paid to do what he'd always wanted to do. Oh dear, he wondered, how long did it take for my attitude to change . . . ?

After the Company Manager, other members of the Pinero resident staff were introduced. The Stage Manager, dour in the manner of all Stage Managers. The Assistant Stage Managers, bright-eyed and bushy-tailed. The Lighting Director, introverted and technical. The Wardrobe Mistress, a symphony in hand-woven fabrics (which didn't fill Charles with confidence —if there was one thing he hated on stage, it was a costume that tickled).

Then the Catering Manager, Norman Phipps, and the Box Office Manager, Sandra, were introduced. She put in the customary plea that the cast give her as much notice as possible for any complimentary or first night tickets they wanted, and made the customary complaint that if they left it to the last minute it not only made her job very difficult, but also caused disappointment and bad feeling.

She had dressed up more for the occasion than for the previous Saturday, but her clothes were again just on the decent side of tarty. This time it was black leather trousers and a cotton loose-knit sleeveless sweater.

And again it wasn't just her dress that was sexy. She also peppered her talk with a few innuendoes, and reacted flirtatiously to questions from the actors. Again, as he had on the Saturday, Charles wondered how much of this was just talk and how much of it she might put into action. Of course, with a constant supply of actors through the theatre, most of whom were enduring long separations from wives and girlfriends, she was in a good position to have plenty of little flings if she wanted them. And, if her relationship with her husband was as bad as she implied, then she might be tempted to indulge herself.

And yet something in Charles doubted it. Her sexuality was so upfront, so aggressively emphatic, that he couldn't believe in it. He felt it was probably all talk, just part of her manner, her personal way of facing the world around her.

The next person to be introduced was the Designer, who spoke at great length about the totally new concept of theatre represented by his set, but whose description of it sounded to Charles exactly like 90 per cent of the sets on which he had strutted in doublet, hose, toga and armour, giving voice to the words of the immortal Bard.

When you cut through the exotic description, all there was going to be onstage was, as usual, a set of battlements at the back, and a pair of mobile towers which could be wheeled on and off for relevant scenes. The outlines of all the crenellations would be sufficiently vague, so that, with a few lighting changes, they could represent A Desert Heath, A Camp Near Forres, Inverness—A Court Within the Castle, The Same —Another Room in the Palace, A Cavern, Fife—Macduff's Castle, Dunsinane, Birnham Wood, The Same—Another Part of the Plain, and so on. Charles felt infinitely old, a Struldbrug of the theatre, who had seen everything and heard everything an infinite number of times before.

"But, now," said Gavin Scholes, once everyone down to the Stage Doorman had been introduced, "the play itself . . ."

A little murmur of excitement went round the cast. It wasn't that they were necessarily excited; it was just that Gavin had delivered his words in a manner that demanded a little murmur of excitement.

"Now, as I see it, *Macbeth* is the tragedy of a man without imagination, whose life is suddenly shaken to the core by the introduction of an imaginative dimension."

"Ah," said George Birkitt blankly. "That sounds very interesting."

Encouraged, Gavin went on, "Lady Macbeth, of course, from the start, has had this imaginative dimension. She is the more intuitive of the pair. She reacts instinctively, whereas Macbeth's reactions are more intellectual . . ."

"But surely," objected the deeply vibrant voice of Felicia Chatterton, "hers is the intellectual approach. I mean, she has the detachment, the cold-bloodedness if you like, to take an overall view, while Macbeth only responds minute by minute."

"Erm . . ." said the director.

"I mean, the first time we see Lady Macbeth, when she's reading the letter, she refers back to conversations about Macbeth's chances of becoming King . . ."

"Yes, yes . . . but—"

"So she is the one who's doing the long-term planning. She is the one who thinks things out intellectually. It's only when Macbeth becomes King that he starts doing things off his own bat."

"Erm . . ."

"You know, the murder of Banquo, the massacre of the Macduff family . . ."

"Yah . . . but—"

"But he's still only reacting minute by minute. Like an animal, covering his tracks. He doesn't think the murder through. Each crime is just a cover-up for the previous one. I think there are very valid parallels with Watergate, you know."

"Yes, yes, I'm sure. But if you could just let me spell out in a bit more detail the way I see the play . . ."

"But I do think it's important that we all see the play the same way. I mean, we really should find its intellectual pivot before we get into rehearsals."

"Oh, I do agree, Felicia. I do agree. But I think what we've got to—"

"Oh, for Christ's sake," boomed Warnock Belvedere. "Let's just bloody get on with it. Acting's nothing to do with bloody talking about the words, it's just standing still, being audible and not bumping into the furniture."

This paraphrase of another of the late Sir Ralph Richardson's dicta was greeted by relieved laughter, and Gavin Scholes took the opportunity to redirect the conversation. "Look, actually, Felicia, I think you've raised some very valid points there, which we certainly must discuss . . . if we have time. But I think if I could start by giving you all my views on the play, and, you know, if you could hear me out, then we could make the discussion more general once I've finished. How do you feel about that?"

"Absolutely fine," Felicia Chatterton agreed very reasonably. "I hope you don't mind if I take notes . . . ?"

"Erm, no, no." Gavin cleared his throat. "Well, er . . . *Macbeth*, as I say, is a play about imagination—or rather, perhaps I should say, it's a play about lack of imagination. Or perhaps both imagination and the lack of it . . ."

Mentally, Charles switched off again. In his experience, directors' theories of plays soon got abandoned in the face of the purely logistical problems of rehearsal. Getting the cast on and off stage quickly took priority over the overall concept of the piece.

He'd only been in one production in his life where a director had followed a single interpretation through from first read-through to first night, and that had been a disaster.

The director in question had seen *The Tempest* as a fantasy taking place inside Prospero's mind. There was nothing wrong with the idea itself; indeed many directors have moved towards that kind of interpretation. Nor was there anything inherently wrong with having a set in the shape of a hollowed-out cranium. Charles really only began to part company with the concept when he saw the costume designs, and realized that all the characters except for Prospero himself were to be dressed as brain-cells.

The director's ideas then got even more convoluted, and he started dividing the cast into different kinds of brain cells, according to which of Prospero's functions they controlled. Ariel was deemed to control the Visual Area, Caliban the Taste Area, Miranda the Sensory Speech Area, and so on. At the play's climax, the lines, "But this rough magic I here abjure", Prospero was instructed by the director to have a stroke, thus killing off certain of the other characters (in their roles as brain-cells), and making the principal actor play the rest of the action with slurred speech and one side of his body paralysed.

It was grotesque, it ran counter to Shakespeare's text at almost every point, but at least the director stuck to his guns and saw it through.

And Charles Paris hadn't done too badly out of it. From press notices of universal condemnation, he, by the good fortune of having one of the smallest parts (that of the Shipmaster) had culled the following review:

42

"Charles Paris was easily the most effective performer on the stage, chiefly because we saw least of him."

It was one of those notices which, if you snip off the second half of the sentence, looks very good in a scrap-book.

Gavin Scholes concluded his exposition of the way he saw *Macbeth* and announced, "Well, now I think we'd better get straight on with the reading, don't you?"

"Surely we're going to discuss the interpretation first?" Needless to say, this bewildered objection came from Felicia Chatterton.

"No, no, I'd rather come to it fresh."

"Oh." This clearly didn't sound a very good idea to her, but she suppressed further objections.

"Erm . . . now, inevitably, with such a big cast we're going to be into a bit of doubling. Now I've cleared extra parts with some of you . . ."

Charles and John B. Murgatroyd chuckled knowingly.

"Some parts I'm cutting. For instance, I've divided Angus's lines up between Lennox, Ross and Mentieth . . ."

"Gosh," whispered John B. to Charles in a voice that had overtones of Felicia Chatterton. "That could be tricky. I mean, I'll have to *talk* Lennox and *think* Angus."

"Then the Fourth Murderer," Gavin went on, "I've assimilated into the other three, and of course I've cut Hecate—"

"Have you?" asked Felicia Chatterton, shocked.

"Yes. Well, everyone cuts Hecate."

"The recent R.S.C. production didn't."

"No, well, I mean everyone in the real world—" He thought better of finishing his sentence and said hastily, "Anyway, I've cut her."

"But surely that removes any occult frame of reference for the Weird Sisters."

"Well, yes, I suppose it . . ." Gavin looked totally nonplussed. "Yes, well, I'm afraid we're just going to have to live with that," he concluded firmly.

"Hmm. Well, if you don't feel you're shortchanging the audience . . ."

"No, I don't. Now a few more doublings. Charles, I know you're already giving us your Bleeding Sergeant and your Drunken Porter . . . would you mind adding a couple more snippets . . . ?"

"No problem. The more the merrier."

"Right. Well, if you could do the Old Man who talks to Ross . . . ?"

"Sure."

"And the Third Murderer . . ."

"Fine."

"Um, and the English Doctor . . . you know, the one who comes in and talks about Edward the Confessor . . . ?"

"Okay."

"Oh, aren't you going to cut that bit?" asked Felicia Chatterton.

"No." Gavin looked uncertain. "Why? Do you think I should?"

"No. No, goodness, no, it's terribly important in terms of the definition of Kingship."

"Yes. Exactly," Gavin agreed, thinking on his feet. "That's why I'm keeping it in."

"Good. Just a lot of directors do cut that bit."

"Not me," said Gavin Scholes smugly. "Very important, the definition of Kingship. Then of course there's the other Doctor . . ." he went on hesitantly, ". . . the Scottish Doctor, the Doctor of Physick in the Sleepwalking Scene. It's a natural doubling with Duncan, actually. Often done. I was wondering, Warnock, whether you might possibly . . .?"

"No." The word was loud and unambiguous.

"But it would be a great help if—"

"No. I am Warnock Belvedere and Warnock Belvedere does not double. I was engaged to play Duncan in this production of *Macbeth*, and that is the only part I intend to play."

"Ah." Gavin hesitated for a moment, as if contemplating

44

remonstrance. But his nerve gave, and once again he turned to where he knew he would get a more accommodating response. "Erm, in that case, Charles, I wonder if you'd mind . . ."

Eventually, the readthrough started. Felicia Chatterton wanted to stop and discuss each line as it came up, but grudgingly conceded agreement that they'd do one straight readthrough and then start talking.

The reading demonstrated a marked contrast in styles between the two principals. Felicia, in spite of wanting to discuss interpretation so much, had already done a great deal of homework. For a start, she knew the lines. And she spoke them with enormous skill and passion, utilizing the full range of her magnificent voice.

George Birkitt, by contrast, gave an appalling reading. He appeared never to have seen or heard any of the lines before in his life and, from some of the readings he gave, certainly not to understand them. Even famous quotations were delivered with leaden incomprehension. George Birkitt's approach to intonation seemed to be based on the simple rule that all personal pronouns should be emphasized. "*I* have done the deed." "How now, you secret, black, and midnight hags! What ist *you* do?" Even "*She* should have died hereafter."

There was also a problem of volume. Not only did George stumble, he also mumbled. He was used to the intimacy of television, where, with microphones continuously poised above the actors' heads, there was no need for projection. Obviously he was going to have to be reminded what it was like to work in the theatre.

But the actor himself did not seem worried by his bad reading. There was no embarrassment as he fluffed and floundered through some of the most famous lines in the English language. Charles was going to be very interested to see how that particular performance grew in the course of rehearsal.

The rest of the cast read predictably. Russ Lavery's Fleance was way over the top, clearly the product of much detailed agonizing in front of his mirror.

Warnock Belvedere was also over the top, but with a chilling authority. From his first line,

"What bloody man is that?",

he dominated his scenes, and Charles, the bloody man in question, looked forward with interest to sharing what was left of the stage with him.

The reading went through jerkily, but without major interruptions, until they broke for coffee at the end of Act Three. The only long silence in the second half occurred in the Apparition Scene. The first Witch cued the first manifestation (an Apparition of an Armed Head) with the line, "He knows thy thought: Hear his speech, but say thou nought", and nothing happened.

"Erm . . ." said Gavin vaguely. "Oh, sorry, haven't I cast this? I wonder, Charles, would you mind . . . ?"

As he read the lines, Charles Paris reflected on the ambiguity of his agent's words about Gavin being "optimistic that there could be some other good parts."

Charles had blithely assumed that that had meant parts in future productions. From the way things were going, it looked as if they all would be in *Macbeth*.

Chapter Four

AFTER THE READTHROUGH they broke for lunch. The theatre was some way out of the town, so most of the company ate and drank in Norman's bar, where a pair of motherly ladies dispensed salads and one hot dish (Irish stew that Monday) from behind an angled glass counter.

Charles Paris joined John B. Murgatroyd and a group of other small-part actors for a good giggle about past theatrical disasters. Warnock Belvedere still held court to a circle of admirers, regaling them with further apocryphal anecdotes of theatrical giants, and drinking far more brandy than seemed suitable for an actor proposing to work in the afternoon.

Gavin Scholes, not surprisingly, found himself monopolized by Felicia Chatterton. But, recognizing that he was going to have to hear her views on the true meaning of *Macbeth* at some point, he shrewdly decided to give up his lunch hour and get them out of the way quickly.

When the company reassembled in the auditorium at two, however, he made it clear that there was not time for further discussion.

During the break, the ASMs had marked out the stage, showing the proportions of the fixed sets, and had assembled a selection of tables and chairs to represent the moving parts. Gavin Scholes moved to the centre of a stage that looked like a furniture warehouse and clapped his hands for attention.

"Erm . . . Okay, everyone, now we're going to block the play through from the start. We'll get on as quickly as possible, so please I must ask none of you to leave the theatre premises, because I don't want any delays. Go to your dressing rooms, by all means. Or the Green Room. Out on the terrace, if you like.

But, please, be somewhere where the ASMs can find you. Okay? Right."

He reached round for a ring-file on a chair and opened it, revealing the text of Shakespeare's play, interleaved with blank pages. "Okay. 'Act One Scene One. A desert heath.' Could I have the Three Witches up here, pronto? Come on love, leave your knitting, cut the cackle. We've got work to do."

"But, Gavin . . ." came a predictable husky voice from the auditorium.

"Yes, Felicia love?" Already there was a hint of strain in his voice. He had listened to her right through lunchtime and he felt he'd done his duty by her. From now on he couldn't afford the time to be so accommodating.

"You aren't really going to start blocking now, are you, Gavin?"

"That's exactly what I'm going to do, yes."

"But we haven't discussed the characters."

"You and I spent all lunchtime discussing the characters."

"But that's only scratched the surface. And we can't start making decisions about where the characters are going to move until we know who those characters are, can we?"

"So what do you suggest we do?"

"Well, I suggest . . . I'd assumed that we'd talk through the characters for a bit, try to sort out their interrelationships . . ."

"For how long?"

"Oh, only a week."

"A week! Out of a three-and-a-half week rehearsal period? You've got to be joking. What, a whole week before we start blocking any of the moves?"

"But once we know who the characters are, then the moves will arise instinctively. We'll know where to go because we'll know who we are."

"I'm sorry, Felicia." Gavin tapped his ring-file. "All the moves are in here."

"What, you mean you've actually worked them out before we've started rehearsing?" she asked, appalled.

48

"Exactly. And I'm afraid, given the time-scale that we have, that is the only way we can possibly get the production ready for the opening."

"But—"

"Sorry, Felicia. We're already ten minutes late starting." And he turned his back on her. "Erm, Witches. Okay . . . Right, I know the text says, 'Enter Three Witches', but I want to have you discovered when the tabs go up. Okay? So let's have you centre stage and . . ."

Charles saw Felicia turn in bewilderment and ask, to no one in particular, "Does he always work like this?"

"I should bloody well hope so," snapped Warnock Belvedere, sprawled bad-temperedly across a seat beside her. "About the one good thing so far you can say for him as a director is that he seems prepared to just get on with it."

"But how can you make a move that doesn't feel right?" she asked in plaintive incomprehension.

"You can make any move you're told to, so long as you're visible to the audience." Warnock fixed the flower of the RSC with a bloodshot eye. "And let me tell you, theatre was a damned sight healthier before everyone started bloody intellectualizing about it. First, the directors began taking the text apart. Now we've got bloody pea-brained actresses turning academic on us."

"But—"

"When I started in the theatre," he continued inexorably, "actresses knew their bloody place—which was either getting up there and saying the lines, or getting down there on their backs and giving the actors what they wanted. They didn't fart on about characterization and motivation."

"So what you're saying is—"

"What I'm saying is just be thankful you're in work and keep your bloody mouth shut!"

There was no ambiguity about this rudeness, and the offence was compounded by the fact that some of Warnock's circle of sycophants sniggered at his words. The colour drained from

Felicia Chatterton's face; she turned and moved with dignity to the back of the auditorium.

On stage, Gavin Scholes pretended he hadn't heard the altercation and continued studiously showing the Three Witches where to move. The blocking of the short scene was quickly completed, the Witches ran it a second time following the pencilled notes they had made in their scripts, and then the director was ready for the next scene.

"Okay. 'Act One Scene Two. A Camp near Forres.' Let's have you on stage, please, Duncan, Malcolm, Donalbain . . . oh, and this is Lennox, isn't it? Come on, John B. and Charles. Bleeding Sergeant."

The Bleeding Sergeant and Lennox rose to their feet and moved forward.

"No, loves, no. You stay there. I want you to make your entrance from the auditorium."

Oh God, thought Charles. All the old tricks. Gavin Scholes really was a boringly traditional director. The predictable set, all the moves worked out in his interleaved script (moves which, Charles knew, would always end up, whenever there were more than three characters on stage, in the time-honoured theatrical semicircle). And entrances from the auditorium. How corny.

In a flash Charles saw exactly what the finished production would be like—a faithful telling of the story, no controversy, no excitement, ideal Schools Matinee fodder.

"Right, so, Duncan, you enter downstage left."

"Downstage?" echoed Warnock Belvedere.

"Yes."

"I think not."

"But—"

"Duncan is a King. The natural place for a King to enter is through the upstage centre archway."

"Erm, yes, except that that entrance is going to represent various castles in—"

"This is where I will enter," announced Warnock Belvedere, stationing himself firmly upstage centre.

"Well, I suppose that'd be all right if—"

"I'll have some attendants, won't I?"

"Well, you'll have Malcolm and Donalbain . . ."

"What about Lennox?"

"No, I've got Lennox helping on the Bleeding Sergeant."

"Surely the Bleeding Sergeant can come on on his own. He's not bleeding that much."

"No, I'm sorry."

Warnock Belvedere sniffed his disapproval. "Oh well, I suppose these two will have to do. Right, we'll try the entrance."

Duncan, followed by Malcolm and Donalbain, disappeared through a break in the curtains at the back of the stage. There was a long pause, during which a muttered confabulation could be heard, then the curtains parted to admit Malcolm and Donalbain, who took up positions either side of the entrance.

After another pause, Duncan swept in. His two sons bowed as he moved centre stage. He looked slowly round the auditorium, then demanded in a booming voice, "'What bloody man is that?'"

"Erm . . ." Gavin Scholes' voice strayed tentatively up from the front row.

"What?"

"I think that's fine . . . I mean, as a move . . ."

"Of course it is."

"But, er, Warnock, if you could say the line as you come in, rather than waiting till you've taken up your position . . .?"

"Why?"

"Well, you know, it's just pace, love, pace. I mean, particularly at the beginning of the show, we do want it to move along. Can't have too long a pause."

"Are you suggesting," asked Warnock Belvedere, puffing himself up with affront, "that I do not know how to judge the length of a pause?"

"No, no."

"I tell you, Noel Coward himself—Noel Coward, no less —admitted that he couldn't hold a candle to me when it came to timing . . ."

"Yes, yes, of course, but—"

"And Tony Guthrie once said to me . . ."

"Heigh-ho. It's going to be like this all the time," John B. Murgatroyd whispered to Charles, with a tremor of a giggle in his voice.

"Best spectator sport since Christians being thrown to the lions," Charles murmured back.

On stage the diatribe continued, until Gavin once again crumbled and agreed to let Warnock do it his way. Then the director turned to the auditorium to direct the entrance of the Bleeding Sergeant.

Following instructions, Lennox supported the wounded man up the centre steps on to the stage.

"I think they'd bow now," said Duncan.

"I'm not sure . . ."

"Duncan is a King, Kevin . . ."

"Gavin."

"Kevin, Gavin, what the hell? They'd bow."

"I don't know . . . Well, okay, try it, Charles and John B."

They collapsed on to the floor, and Charles could feel the silent vibration of John B. Murgatroyd giggling beside him. Oh dear. He suddenly remembered that John B. was one of the worst corpsers in the business. They were going to be lucky to get through this scene every night without breaking up.

Malcolm then stepped forward and instructed the Bleeding Sergeant to "say to the King the knowledge of the broil

As thou didst leave it."

Charles began, "'Doubtful it stood:

As two spent swimmers, that do—'"

"Erm, I think we'd better have you standing for this, Charles. Want the audience to see you a bit, don't we?"

"I don't see the necessity," boomed Warnock Belvedere.

Well, sod you, thought Charles. See if I care. At least if I keep my back to them throughout the scene, it'll save another make-up change.

Rehearsals did progress through the week. They slipped behind a bit, but, considering the ridiculous schedule Gavin was trying to keep to, the slippage could have been a lot worse.

Warnock Belvedere, having imposed his personality on the company to his satisfaction, seemed to calm down a bit. Or perhaps it was just that he wasn't around so much. Duncan, as Charles had observed, gets killed satisfactorily early in the play and so, since they were working through from the beginning, Warnock was soon free while the rest of the blocking continued. He wasn't called for either the Wednesday or the Thursday's rehearsals. And, without his malevolent presence, the mood of the company improved.

Felicia, too, stopped making objections and buckled down to hard work. Accepting that she was not going to be allowed to discover movements that arose naturally from her discovery of her character, she began instead to devote her considerable powers of concentration to making Gavin's imposed moves fit into her developing concept of Lady Macbeth.

She also found a confidant in Russ Lavery, whose earnestness matched her own, and who was evidently more than happy to spend long hours agonizing with her over nuances of Shakespeare's text. This new friendship was a great blessing to Gavin Scholes, because it got Felicia off his back.

Her attitude towards the director changed. Whereas at first she had been trying to challenge his methods of production, now she seemed to feel only pity for his philistinism, sorrow that the fine workmanship of the Bard should have to suffer at the clumsy hands of such a botcher. But at least she didn't stop to argue every point, and the rehearsals were allowed to proceed.

George Birkitt also got better, but slowly. He still had a great many television habits to shake off. Apart from the problem of projection, he was also having considerable difficulty implanting Shakespeare's immortal lines in his mind. Actors in television sit coms are notorious paraphrasers, who give rough approximations of their lines, only homing in with accuracy on the ones which are likely to get laughs. For someone used to that discipline, it was a considerable challenge to have to repeat lines which half the world knew off by heart (and which, at Schools Matinees, might even be being followed in the script by the light of pencil torches).

For a couple of days, George floundered hopelessly. The lines just would not stick. It was only when Charles Paris gently reminded him of a play called *The Hooded Owl* that a marked improvement was seen. They had both been in the first production of the piece, in which the star, Michael Banks, unable to remember his lines, had had to go through the ignominy of having them fed to him from the wings through a radio receiver disguised as a hearing aid. The threat of a repeat of this procedure soon bucked George up—apart from anything else, the presence of a hearing aid in eleventh century Scotland would be difficult to explain away.

Once the lines had started to come, the performance grew. George had a good stage presence and, when he bothered to use it, a strong voice. And in one respect his television training proved useful. Recognizing (though not admitting) that he had no instinctive ear for a comic line, he had always been quite happy to parrot intonations given him by sit com directors. Once Gavin Scholes realized that George was not offended by being told how to say the lines—in fact, even welcomed it—the director took full advantage of the concession. Whatever George Birkitt's limitations as a creative actor may have been, he had a great ability for copying an intonation. So the director spoke the lines as he wanted them delivered, George reproduced the director's emphases, and slowly a performance emerged.

The pairing of this Macbeth and Lady Macbeth was unusual, the one a mere parrot of lines, the other unable to deliver a line that had not been dissected and reassembled half a dozen times, but, though their routes to it could not have been more different, both arrived at a remarkably consistent style.

Another problem with George Birkitt, however, was that he, the member of the cast who needed most rehearsal, was going to have least. The filming days for his new sit com, so carefully negotiated into his contract, would take him out of *Macbeth* rehearsals for two full days.

And that was not all. On the Wednesday of the first week, Gavin Scholes for the first time outlined his longer-term rehearsal plan.

"What we're working towards," he said, "with all this manic blocking, is a full runthrough of the play on Saturday."

The shock of this proposal was so great to her that Felicia Chatterton could not help reacting. "*This* Saturday?"

"Yes."

"A full run? After five days' rehearsal?"

"Yes. Just to fix the blocking in your minds. It won't really be a full runthrough. More a staggerthrough."

"A drunken lurchthrough for Warnock, no doubt," John B. Murgatroyd whispered to Charles, with a giggle.

"Yes," Gavin went on. "We've got to try it. See how the play hangs together. Not too rushed, though. First half Saturday morning, second half in the afternoon."

"Ah," George Birkitt interposed.

"Some problem, George?"

"Yes. Saturday afternoon. No can do."

"What?"

"Didn't the agent tell you?"

"No."

"God, he's hopeless. The money I pay him and . . . No, I've got to fly to Paris for filming on Sunday. Flight late Saturday afternoon. Car picking me up here at one."

"Oh."

"I'm sure the agent must've mentioned it."

"I don't think so."

George Birkitt shrugged. "Well, sorry, old chum. 'Fraid that's the way it is."

"So it sounds as if we can't have a full runthrough on Saturday." Felicia Chatterton sighed with relief.

"Oh yes, we can," Gavin Scholes countered. "We'll do the whole play Saturday morning."

Felicia Chatterton's mouth gaped in pained disbelief. It had never been like this at Stratford.

By the Thursday afternoon, rehearsals were starting to slip behind schedule again. They were doing the Apparition Scene which, since Gavin was not resorting to any stylization but doggedly insisted on all the manifestations being seen by the audience, was very complicated.

Gavin's little drawings of movements in his interleaved script somehow didn't match the size of the stage for this scene, and the problems of getting the apparitions on and off unseen required a major rethink of his plans. He kept saying, "There'll be lots of dry ice. And with proper lighting the audience won't notice a thing", but the cast weren't convinced. They'd all, at some time or other in their careers, been caught in some ungainly posture on an ill-conceived entrance or exit, and none of them wanted to get laughs of that kind again.

So, while the scene was rethought, time passed and they slipped further and further behind schedule.

"I'm sorry," Gavin said after a while. "I can't concentrate in here. Just give me a quarter of an hour—break for tea—and I'll go and work it out in the office."

The cast all trooped up to the bar, where Norman's motherly ladies dispensed tea and rock cakes. Charles sat down at a table with John B. Murgatroyd, who suddenly asked, "Have you ever played the Walnut Game?"

"I don't think so. What is it?"

"It's an old actor's game. Has to be in a play with a big cast. Shakespeare's ideal."

"What happens?"

56

"It's a matinee game. Or late into a run. When the director's not monitoring the performances too closely." John B. Murgatroyd winked.

"What do you have to do?"

"Somebody comes on stage with a walnut and secretly . . . you know, in a handshake or something, they pass it to another actor. Then he has to pass it on. The aim is to keep it on stage throughout the show."

"Just passing it from one to the other?"

"That's it. You lose if you're the one who takes it offstage." Charles smiled mischievously. "Sounds wicked."

"Must try it one day." John B. Murgatroyd looked innocently out of the window.

"If you're thinking what I think you're thinking," said Charles, "be advised. There are one or two people in this company who wouldn't see the joke at all."

"Felicia . . . ?"

"To name but one."

"She wouldn't see a joke if it knocked her over and raped her."

"No. Sad, isn't it, really," Charles mused, "that someone so amazingly dishy should be utterly devoid of humour."

"Tragic," John B. agreed. "I wonder what she does for sex . . . ?"

"Talks about it, I'm sure. At length. At great, great length."

"You don't think young Russ is getting anywhere there?"

"No." Charles lengthened the vowel in disbelief.

But further speculation about Felicia's sex-life was interrupted by the arrival of Sandra Phipps, with a shy-looking schoolboy in tow.

"Charles, I wonder, do you mind? Could you just keep an eye on Stewart?"

"Sure. No problem."

"I've been with him all afternoon, but I must go and check what's going on in the Box Office."

"Fine."

57

"You see, I'm meant to be chaperoning him . . ."

"Of course."

"The law says kids have got to have chaperons. Good old Gavin, always ready to save a few bob, says, 'Why book anyone else when we've got Mum on the premises?' so I'm doing it."

"Don't worry. I'll see he doesn't get into any mischief. Do you want a drink, Stewart?"

The boy looked up at him through long lashes. He was still at a downy girlish stage of boyhood, just before his skin would coarsen and his beard start.

"I wouldn't mind a Coke, please, if that's all right, sir," the boy replied politely.

"Sure. But please don't call me 'sir'. Charles is fine."

Sandra looked at her watch. "I won't be long. How late do you go on?"

"Half-past five . . . six."

"Stewart was called for two."

"Running late. The murder of the Macduffs is the next scene, though."

"Hmm. You think Gavin'll get to it today?"

"I know he's hoping to."

But Charles's optimistic prediction proved incorrect. They worked on the blocking of the Apparition Scene (which now involved much use of the stage trap-door) for the rest of the afternoon. When they broke, the director shouted out, "Okay. Thanks for all your hard work. Macduff murder scene prompt at ten in the morning—okay?"

"Is that okay for you?" Charles asked the boy sitting beside him in the auditorium. "I mean, with school?"

"Oh, I'm sure it'll be all right."

"Where are you at school?"

"St. Joseph's."

The name didn't mean anything to Charles. But then the name of none of the local schools would have meant anything to him. Stupid question to ask, really.

"Hey, that's great," said Stewart. "It means I'll miss Double English."

"From your tone of voice, that's pretty boring."

"And how!" The boy grimaced. "Bor*ing*."

"Why? What are you doing?"

"*Macbeth*," Stewart Phipps replied with a groan.

Chapter Five

THEY DID MANAGE to get the whole play blocked by the end of rehearsal on the Friday, but only by dint of going into overtime. Most of them worked through till just after eight, because virtually the entire cast was involved in the battle scenes at the end. (Charles, incidentally, had picked up a couple more parts here—one of the soldiers in Malcolm's army who grabs a bit of Birnham Wood, and then, with a change of allegiance which might have confused an actor of more Stanislavskian approach, one of Macbeth's army who runs away as the tide of battle turns.)

All the cast logged in their overtime with the theatre administration. To Charles this still seemed strange. Though he approved of much of what Equity had done to improve actors' working conditions, and though he always welcomed a little extra money, this unionized clock-watching seemed dangerously closer to the world of the Civil Service than the theatre. Charles felt wistfully nostalgic for the days of weekly rep. Then you worked ridiculous hours, you moaned and groaned and complained about it all the time, but the feeling of mutual exhaustion kept everyone on a permanent high, pumping adrenalin at a rate he had never since encountered.

Still, those days were gone. Now there were rules fixing the permissible hours of work, and those rules had to be obeyed.

Stewart Phipps' scene was blocked first thing on the Friday morning, as Gavin had intended. It didn't take long. Stewart spoke the rather prissy lines of Macduff's Son with commendable animation, and was clearly going to relish the moment of his death, when he was despatched by John B. Murgatroyd (as the First Murderer) with the immortal words,

"What! you egg, Young fry of treachery!"

But the boy didn't leave straight after his scene. The theatrical atmosphere patently excited him, and he gazed from the auditorium with sparkling eyes, taking in everything that was going on.

"Shouldn't you be getting back to school?" Charles asked just before they broke for lunch, but the boy said, "No. They won't mind. They aren't to know how long I'm actually needed for rehearsal."

Charles shrugged. It wasn't his business. And Sandra Phipps, whose business in her dual role of mother and chaperon it certainly was, spent most of the day in the Box Office and was either unaware of, or unworried by, her son's continuing presence.

So, by the end of the Friday, every move in the play had been gone through at least once. All was set for the Saturday morning runthrough—though the less optimistic definitions of staggerthrough, lurchthrough, hobblethrough, stumblethrough or even tumblethrough, became increasingly likely to be apt.

The advantage of doing a full run so prematurely was that at least everyone in the cast got an idea of what they were up against.

Felicia Chatterton, who had given up remonstrating about the folly of running the play so soon, approached the exercise with her customary seriousness, and was to be found at ninethirty on the Saturday morning in the middle of the stage, working through a series of yoga postures and breathing exercises. She felt that proper preparation was always essential in acting, even just for a first run.

Beside her on the stage, shadowing her every movement, and with his face set in an expression of equal reverence, was her faithful dog—or perhaps puppy—Russ Lavery.

The other actors who trickled into the auditorium may have grinned covertly at what they saw on stage, but at least they restrained themselves from outright sniggering. Though they didn't all favour such intensity of approach for themselves, they were a tolerant lot. If that's how Felicia wanted to work, fair enough, it didn't cause any trouble.

"Oh, Christ love," hissed John B. Murgatroyd to Charles in a voice of agonized campness, "how can Gavin expect me to give a performance at this kind of notice? My body-clock's all set wrong for a start. And then, although I did all my Lennox exercises before I left the digs, I just haven't had time to do my First Murderer workout."

"You think you've got problems, sweetie," Charles murmured back in matching style. "I tell you, I've been up half the night. First, I had to do my Bleeding Sergeant build-up, then my Drunken Porter build-up . . ."

"Must be hell getting yourself into that part."

"Yes, character acting's always difficult. Then I had to do my Third Murderer exercises, then the English Doctor, then . . ."

They both subsided into stifled giggles.

But once the run started, Charles was made aware of the problems that his multiplicity of parts caused. Not acting problems—he could come up with a sufficient variety of accents and postures with no effort at all—but purely logistical problems. The blocking rehearsals had taken the play scene by scene; it was only when the whole thing was linked together that the difficulties of so many entrances and exits became apparent.

It soon became clear that Charles Paris would spend almost the entire play running at full tilt round the back of the stage.

As the Bleeding Sergeant, he entered from the auditorium and exited downstage right (had to be downstage—in any scene featuring Duncan, only Warnock Belvedere got upstage exits). Then, in Act One Scene Seven, Charles had to enter upstage left and cross over to exit upstage right. (Yes, the worst had happened—he'd also been lumbered with the part of that bloody Sewer.) As the Drunken Porter, he entered and exited downstage left. As the Old Man who talked to Ross in Act Two Scene Four, he entered and exited upstage right. The Third Murderer, like the Bleeding Sergeant, entered through the auditorium and, after the despatch of Banquo, went off upstage left.

There was then a brief respite, which encompassed the interval (Gavin Scholes had predictably followed the traditional practice of placing this immediately after the Banquet Scene), until Charles had to give his Apparition of an Armed Head. For this, following Gavin's rethink, he made his entrance through a trap door under the stage, to emerge in a haze of dry ice through the Witches' cauldron (assuming that this particular bit of stage magic worked—an assumption which, at that point, only the director was making with any confidence). The Apparition vanished the same way he'd come.

The Third Murderer was once again enlisted to help massacre the Macduff family, and for this occasion he entered and exited downstage left. The English Doctor, whose four-and-a-half lines were so pertinent in the definition of Kingship, entered and exited upstage right. The Scottish Doctor brought in as a consultant on the Lady Macbeth sleepwalking case, also entered and exited upstage right.

From there on, Charles was into acting soldiers on one side or the other in the final conflict, and for these the entrances and exits (sometimes with and sometimes without chunks of Birnham Wood) were respectively downstage left, upstage right, from the auditorium, upstage left, downstage left and upstage left.

Basically, it seemed to Charles that each performance would qualify as a heavy training session for a decathlete.

And that was before he started thinking about costume and make-up changes.

The Pinero Theatre, Warminster, was only about twenty years old, and of an attractive and intelligent design. Its one drawback was its location which, though it commanded beautiful views over towards Salisbury Plain, was too far out of town for economic health. It was not a theatre which shoppers would pass; anyone who wanted to go and see a play had to make a special expedition. This did not help in the crazy game of knife-edge juggling by which most theatres manage their financial affairs. Arts Council and local council grants come and go, lucrative transfers from the provinces to the West End are rare, and the basic survival of a theatre depends on the time-honoured resource, much cited by Gavin Scholes, of "putting bums on seats". In achieving this, the Pinero was always going to be hampered by its position.

But those who did make the effort to get to the theatre, found a welcoming environment. They entered a large, glass-fronted foyer, which housed Sandra Phipps' Box Office. Staircases on either side of this took the visitors up to Norman Phipps' bar, at either end of which were the two main entrances to the auditorium.

The bar was directly above the dressing room area, which was thus behind and under the auditorium rather than in the traditional backstage position. Passages led along the sides of the theatre to the wings, and there were pass-doors at the corners of the auditorium.

In the course of that first Saturday morning runthrough, Charles Paris got to know this geography rather well.

It was a somewhat giggly occasion for those of the company prone to giggling (in other words, everyone except Gavin, who was too busy, and Felicia, who didn't know how to . . . oh, and Russ, whose devotion to Felicia would not allow him to).

Faced with the enormity of the whole play, George Birkitt's performance slipped down the few notches it had so laboriously climbed during the previous week. Apart from anything else, he was distracted; his mind was on the next day's filming in Paris, and he continually glanced at his watch or peered out into the auditorium for the outline of a hire-car chauffeur.

The interval break was brief, because of the pressure of time, and the company struggled into the Green Room to make themselves coffee from an inadequate number of electric kettles. Charles decided to avoid the crush; he'd wait till lunchtime and have a proper drink then. A good few proper drinks. After all, there'd be no more work till the Monday morning. He looked forward to the weekend. A few days before he had contemplated another attempt to make contact with Frances, but since then he'd discovered that John B. Murgatroyd had a car, and they had agreed to devote the break to an in-depth investigation of the pubs of Wiltshire.

As Charles came out of his dressing room, trying to remember what the hell character he had to play next, he encountered Norman Phipps and his son staggering along under the weight of a large metal beer keg. They were carrying it from the delivery door to a small store-room where the bar supplies were kept.

"Can I give you a hand?"

Norman accepted the offer gratefully. "There are three more outside. And a few crates. Why they have to deliver on a Saturday I don't know."

The keg was heavy. Charles took over one end from Stewart and Norman backed into the store-room. "Watch out, Charles. There's a little step down."

They collected the other three. After his multi-character exertions in the first half of *Macbeth*, Charles found he was quite puffed as they wheeled the last keg clattering into position. He leant back against a padlocked cupboard in the store-room.

"Thanks very much," said Norman. Stewart had run off as soon as he saw his father had alternative assistance. The boy seemed to run everywhere. He was in the state of high stagestruck excitement, and, until the moment for his big scene came, just couldn't see enough of what was going on backstage. He seemed to have lost his initial shyness and now chattered away cheerfully to anyone and everyone in the company.

Charles looked around the store-room. There were gas cylinders beside the kegs and from the top of each keg thin translucent tubes ran up to holes in the ceiling.

"That's how the beer gets pumped up?"

Norman nodded, as he clamped the fixture at the end of one

of the tubes on to a new barrel. There was a little hiss of escaping gas. "Yes, for the ones who like their beer fizzy. The Real Ale specialists don't like the idea of CO_2 near their beer. Theirs is done by hand-pumps."

"Do you get much call for Real Ale?"

The Bar Manager shrugged. "Not as much as there was a few years ago. The campaign seems to have died down a bit."

"What do you keep in here?" Charles indicated the pad-locked cupboard.

"Spirits. Can't be too careful. Lots of people come in and out of a theatre."

"Actors, you mean?"

The Bar Manager allowed himself a brief smile. "Not just actors."

At that moment Russ Lavery appeared in the doorway. "Oh, I've often wondered what was in here."

"My stock-room," said Norman Phipps stolidly.

"Don't worry, I recognize it," said Russ. "I've been working as a barman the last couple of years to supplement my grant." He turned to Charles. "They've started the Apparition Scene."

"Oh, I'd better shift. I wonder if they've got the trap working this morning . . ."

Norman Phipps followed him out of the store-room, switching the light off as he came. Then he closed the door, and bent to attach another padlock to the metal rings that fixed it.

"Don't you use the ordinary lock?" asked Charles, indicating a keyhole in the door.

"Broken. This room's been raided more than once."

"Actors?" asked Charles again.

The suggestion got another small smile from Norman. "I didn't say so."

John B. Murgatroyd came bustling up to Charles. "Come on, ready to give your Apparition of an Armed Head?"

"Do you know if the trap's working?"

"You bet. Come on."

In the area under the stage stood a wooden framework which

housed the trap-door mechanism. At the bottom of this was a platform, supported on ropes. It was counterweighted, so that it could be raised quite easily with the full weight of a human being on it. Assistant Stage Managers would pull down on the ropes on the given cue, and the actor on the platform would suddenly appear up on stage. The skill in working the trap lay in controlling the speed of the ascent.

There were no members of the stage management about when Charles and John B. Murgatroyd reached the apparatus. "Are you sure we're meant to be using it for this run?" asked Charles.

"Yes. The ASMs are all tied up at the moment, but they asked me to operate it."

"Oh well, if you say so." Charles stepped gingerly on to the platform as John B. took hold of the rope with both hands.

"What's the cue, Charles?"

"'Come high or low;
Thyself and office deftly show.'"

"Okay." John B. Murgatroyd braced himself. They were silent, listening to the heavy footfalls and muffled voices above their heads. They could hear the whine of the Witches and the booming tones of George Birkitt, but the precise words were difficult to distinguish.

"That's it," said Charles, as he thought he recognized the cue.

"Bon voyage," giggled John B. Murgatroyd, and he gave an almighty heave on the rope.

Charles felt himself shoot up in the air like a rocket. He was aware of the bemused expressions of George Birkitt and the Witches as he burst into view. Then he felt the jolt of the platform beneath him suddenly stopping, and then nothing beneath his feet as his own ascent continued.

Landing back on the platform with a spine-jarring thump, he could hear a wicked, muffled giggle from beneath the stage.

"Sod you, John B. Murgatroyd!" shouted the Apparition of an Armed Head.

*

67

The tone of the run had been fairly giggly before this incident, but after it the floodgates of laughter were released. Hardly any scene passed without a complete break-up amongst the cast. Almost all actors are susceptible to corpsing and, if the director doesn't stamp on it firmly, it can quickly become an epidemic. Gavin Scholes did not have it in his nature to stamp on anything firmly, so the play just seemed to get funnier and funnier to the entire company.

The climax came in Macbeth's final scene. In his confrontation with Macduff, George Birkitt had regained a kind of stature and he was rather impressive as he began his last speech.

"I will not yield,
To kiss the ground before young Malcolm's feet,
And to be baited with the rabble's curse.
Though Birnham Wood be come to Dunsinane,
And thou oppos'd, being of no woman born,
Yet I will try the last: before my body
I will throw my warlike shield. Lay on, Macduff,
And damn'd be he that first cries . . ."

But at this vital juncture, Macbeth's attention wandered. He sighted something at the back of the auditorium and concluded the speech, "Oh, sorry, loves, there's my car, must dash."

This unintentional bathos brought the house down, and under cover of the laughter, George Birkitt made good his escape, ignoring Gavin Scholes' plaintive voice following him with "Could you just hang on for a few notes, love . . . ?"

It was the end of the runthrough, staggerthrough, stumblethrough, tumblethrough or fumblethrough. The director had no hope of reimposing control after that, and he bowed to the inevitable. "Okay, we'd better leave it there. Notes first thing Monday morning. Do look at the lines over the weekend. Don't worry. There are still a few rough edges, but it's coming."

This understatement prompted another round of laughter, and the company adjourned to the bar in a state of high hilarity.

Needless to say, there was one person who did not see the joke.

Felicia Chatterton, a few minutes later, strode through the prattling throng in the bar towards the director, who was just hoping to relax over a glass of wine. Russ Lavery was a rather nervous acolyte in her wake.

"Gavin . . ." she began in a steely voice.

"Yes, love?"

"I'm afraid we can't go on like this."

"What do you mean?"

"This total lack of discipline."

He smiled a smile which had in the past proved disarming. "Yes, okay, I admit this morning was a complete shambles, but you're bound to get one rehearsal like that. Don't worry, everyone's got it out of their system now. We'll really buckle down to it on Monday."

She was not reassured. "I'm afraid I can't act with people who behave like that. I find it impossible to concentrate and build a performance."

"So what are you suggesting?"

"I am suggesting that the disruptive elements are removed from the cast."

"What?"

"Either they go, or I'll have to go."

The director was struck dumb, but another voice took up the challenge.

"Who does she think she is—Sarah Bloody Bernhardt?" Warnock Belvedere sounded even more belligerent than usual. He looked angry and disappointed, and the brandy he clutched was not his first of the morning.

"I just want to work with people who are professional, that's all," Felicia explained reasonably.

This really caught Warnock on the raw. To cast doubts on his professionalism is the worst insult to any actor. "And who are you calling unprofessional, you jumped-up little tart?"

Felicia maintained her dignity. "I am talking about any members of this company who aren't taking the play seriously."

"Like me, for instance?" The old actor was now enjoying baiting her.

"Yes."

"So you're saying that *I* should get out of the company?"

"Yes," she replied evenly. She fixed him with her fierce blue eyes. "One way or another, you've got to go."

Chapter Six

THE SECOND MONDAY of rehearsals was a really bad day. In fact, in the long annals of theatrical disasters, there can have been few to match it.

For Charles Paris it started unfortunately, because he woke up with a grinding hangover. His in-depth investigation of the pubs of Wiltshire with John B. Murgatroyd had perhaps gone in too deep. When they met at the theatre on the Monday, Charles discovered that John B. was in exactly the same condition as he was. Their recollections of the final stages of the previous evening were equally vague.

What made it terrifying in retrospect was that John B. had actually driven them back to their digs.

But two hungover small-part actors did not pose a great threat to Gavin Scholes' rehearsal plans. Indeed, hungover actors at morning rehearsals are such a common occurrence that he hardly noticed their bleariness and slow reactions.

What did throw his schedule into disarray, though, was the phone message that came through at ten-fifteen. George Birkitt was fogbound in Paris. There had been no flights out of the city the previous night and, unless the weather showed a very sudden improvement, there was no chance of his putting in an appearance at that day's rehearsals.

But troubles, as Shakespeare, that well-known provider of platitudes for every occasion, observed in another of his plays, do not often come singly. Before Gavin had had time to digest his first gobbet of bad news, Sandra Phipps came into the theatre to announce that Stewart was no longer going to be allowed to take part in the production.

Apparently his blithe confidence that St. Joseph's School

71

wouldn't mind about his taking the Friday off for rehearsal had been misplaced. Because he hadn't even taken the precaution of telling his form master he would not be present, there had been a heated phone-call to the Phipps' home on the Sunday evening, the upshot of which was that Stewart was forbidden to continue in the play.

So, not only had Gavin Scholes lost his principal actor for an unspecified length of time, he was also faced with the problem of finding another son for Macduff. And he knew how time-consuming booking and licensing juveniles could be.

"Don't you think there's a chance if I rang up St. Joseph's and spoke to the teacher myself, he might relent?" the director asked plaintively.

"No," Sandra replied. "Not in the mood he's in at the moment. In fact, I must ask you, please, not to do it. Stewart's in bad enough odour there already. I think a call from you could only make it worse for him. No, I'm sorry, he's definitely out. His form master only grudgingly allowed him to be in the show in the first place—on the understanding that his work didn't suffer, you know, with his exams coming up. And now . . ." She shrugged helplessly. "He's Head of English, this master, you see, and he's Stewart's English master, and I'm afraid English isn't Stewart's strongest subject."

So that was that. Two-and-a-half weeks to go, and another Macduff's Son needed in a hurry. Oh dear, Gavin thought, probably have to go to a stage school now. And I did specifically want to avoid that. Stage children are so self-consciously theatrical. He looked dejectedly round the auditorium.

When the director's eye lighted on Charles Paris, John B. Murgatroyd leant forward and whispered in his friend's ear. "Watch it. I think he's about to say, 'Charles, I wonder if you'd mind . . . ?' Oh, come on, love, an actor of your wide versatility should have no problem adding the role of a ten-year-old boy to your portfolio . . ."

Charles giggled weakly. But giggling was a bad idea. It only made his head ache more.

To compound the director's problems, Warnock Belvedere arrived at rehearsal late, and in a fouler mood than usual. Something must have happened over the weekend to upset him. He looked mean and disgruntled, and no one escaped the lash of his tongue.

But he kept his most vicious lines for Gavin and Felicia. Once, when the director tried to suggest a change of intonation to him, the old actor snapped out, "Come on, love, make a decision. Do you want me to do the line the way you tell me, or to do it *right*?"

As with most of Warnock's lines, it was not original. Charles had heard it attributed many times to various theatrical luminaries. He had even heard it used once or twice. But never with such belittling venom.

Felicia, too, suffered from Warnock's tongue. When she entered to welcome Duncan to her castle in Act One Scene Six, she stood for a moment locked in thought.

"Get on with it!" Warnock hissed.

"I'm having a lot of difficulty with the delivery," Felicia said thoughtfully.

"Oh, Christ!" Warnock Belvedere swept downstage and boomed out over the stalls, "Is there a bloody midwife in the house?"

Felicia recoiled as if struck in the face, and turned appealingly towards Gavin. The director seemed suddenly to have found something deeply riveting in his script.

The moment passed, but the bad feeling didn't.

From its bad start, the day deteriorated. After the debacle of the Saturday runthrough, Gavin Scholes needed a really hard-working, concentrated rehearsal to re-establish his authority, but the absence of George Birkitt had made that impossible.

Instead, the concentration of the cast wavered. Silly mistakes were made, there was more giggling. But this time it was not a genial hilarity, just a kind of niggling, annoying fooling-around, a joke that had outlived its humour. It was difficult, under the circumstances, to get any constructive work done.

Charles Paris participated in this silliness, which did not improve his mood, but merely increased the self-distaste engendered by his hangover. Then, because it was the only thing likely to make him feel better, he overindulged in the bar at lunchtime. The new drink topped up the old drink of the night before, and he felt quite drunk when he returned for afternoon rehearsal.

It became clear, as the afternoon progressed, that he wasn't the only member of the company in that condition. The silly giggling continued through the rehearsal, until Gavin Scholes was driven to stage an ineffectual and embarrassing tantrum.

Charles felt despicable as the company spirit deteriorated. He could sense the burning resentment of Felicia Chatterton for what was going on, but seemed incapable of turning the tide of childishness in himself, let alone in anyone else.

He knew that actors very rarely behaved so badly. Most of the time they are diligent professionals. But, like anyone else, they need discipline and, in the face of uncertainty and indecision, they can get out of hand. The limpness of Gavin Scholes' manner was doing nothing to put them back on the right track, and Warnock Belvedere seemed to be taking malicious glee in exploiting the situation, constantly pointing up the director's weakness and, presumably by implication, his own strength.

When Gavin finally gave up the unequal struggle and ended the rehearsal soon after five, it was to reactions of universal relief.

But days which start that badly rarely demonstrate sudden improvements. And, true to form, this one got decidedly worse.

Charles knew that the sensible thing to do at the end of rehearsal was to go out and have a brisk walk to clear his head; then go back to his digs for a plain supper and early night.

Equally, he knew that what he would do would be to make

everything worse by hanging around the theatre until Norman's bar opened at six, and then stay there far too long.

Which was exactly what he did.

In fact, he stayed in the bar until closing time.

By then he really was woozy. He hadn't been on a continuous bender like that for some years.

But it had not been a joyous inebriation. It had been one that he knew he would regret, one that he regretted even as he nurtured it. With the looming of each new round, he knew he should stop, quit while he was . . . well, if not exactly ahead, at least not as far behind as he would be if he had another drink.

But each time he weakened and succumbed. A kamikaze recklessness took hold of him, and his own spirits sank as alcoholic spirits fuelled his self-disgust.

John B. Murgatroyd had been with him at the start of the evening, but he, showing better judgement than his friend, had left after a couple of pints.

Charles was not the only member of the company still in the bar when Norman called his impassive "Time". Warnock Belvedere had left only a moment before. Gavin Scholes was sharing his troubles and a bottle of Riesling with Lady Macduff and two of the Witches. And, surprisingly, in a corner booth over a glass of Perrier, Felicia Chatterton remained, vigorously dissecting her art to the unquestioning ear of Russ Lavery.

Alone, her back pointedly turned to the bar and her husband, Sandra Phipps sat, balefully nursing the last dregs of her Tia Maria.

As "Time" was called, Charles, also by now sitting on his own, decided he must go down to his dressing room to fetch his coat and then, finally, get back to his digs. But, as he shifted his bulk off his barstool, the floor seemed suddenly and vindictively to have been moved. He sprawled in an ungainly heap, the barstool tumbling after him.

"Are you okay?"

The figure of Gavin loomed over him. Russ Lavery's anxious face was also just on the edge of his field of vision.

"Yes, yes, I'm fine." Charles knew the words were coming out slurred, and hated himself for it. Without dignity, he pulled himself up against the bar and, in an unsuccessful attempt at insouciance, waved a furry "Goodbye" to the assembled throng before making his ignominious exit.

The stairs to the foyer had taken on the quality of an escalator, and he moved down them gingerly, hand gripping what seemed to be a moving rail. He staggered through the pass-door and strode resolutely but elliptically along the passage.

This involved passing the open door of Warnock Belvedere's dressing room. The old actor's huge body was piled on top of a defenceless plastic chair. He was swigging from a full bottle of Courvoisier, but he cocked his monocled eye at Charles's erratic approach.

Finishing his swallow, he observed with relish, "What a bloody shambles of a day."

"Hear, hear." Charles's hand found the support of the door-frame, which proved to be further away than it looked.

"Nothing you can do with a day like this but get well and truly plastered."

"That," Charles agreed, with a bizarre attempt at poise, "has been my solution to the problem."

"The ideal now, in fact, to complement this bottle . . ." He waved the Courvoisier ". . . would be a nice juicy little bumboy."

"Ah," said Charles.

"Not your sort of thing, is it . . . ? By any chance . . . ?"

In his fuddled state, it took Charles a moment to realize that he was in fact being propositioned. The idea seemed incongruous. He didn't know whether to be flattered or insulted.

But he wasn't too drunk to know that he should refuse the offer. "Sorry," he mumbled apologetically. "'Fraid it's never appealed . . ."

"Ah well," Warnock mused. "Don't know what you've been missing." He took another swig from the bottle. "I'll have to content myself with just the booze." He looked appreciatively at the Courvoisier. "What it is to have a generous friend."

Charles suddenly felt almost faint from weariness. "Must go. Tired out. Just get my coat and . . ."

He eased off the door-frame and propelled himself towards his own dressing room. His eyelids were weighted with lead.

He pushed through the door. The light from the passage illuminated the chair in front of his mirror, and he made towards it without bothering to switch on the dressing room light.

At the third attempt, he slumped into the chair. By then the door, self-closing as the fire regulations demanded, had clicked shut and he was in the dark.

But he didn't mind. He lowered his head gratefully on to the table in front of the mirror and, in a matter of seconds, Charles Paris was asleep.

Chapter Seven

HE WOKE WITH a head like a hornet's nest, a mouth like a blocked drain, and a desperate need to pee.

For a moment he didn't know where he was. The darkness was total. Then, remembering, he felt along the table towards a light switch.

The sudden blaze drove red-hot nails into his eyes. He blinked in agony. Not time to get to the Gents along the passage. He used the wash-basin noisily, comforting himself with the thought that some of the old actor-laddies reckoned that brought good luck.

He swayed erratically until he had overcome the apparently insuperable problem of doing up his zip. Then he looked at his watch.

Ten to three. Ugh. He must get back to his digs.

There was no light in the passage outside. Oh no, the Stage doorman must have thought the theatre was empty, and locked up. God, he might be stuck in there till the morning. That'd give the rest of the company a good laugh, he thought ruefully.

He found a switch in the passage and deluged himself with more scalding light. He made his way gingerly towards the Stage Door, hoping against hope that it might just be secured on a latch that could be opened from the inside.

As he edged along, he noticed that the door to Norman's store-room was open. Curious, he moved closer.

The padlock had not been unlocked, but one of the rings to which it was attached had been wrenched away from the door-frame. The screws still stuck forlornly out of the metal plate.

There was no light in the store-room, so he found the switch and once again light seared his eyeballs.

When he had stopped blinking, he stepped down into the room and looked at the scene that greeted his aching eyes.

The padlock on the spirits cupboard had also been forced, and one or two bottles had crashed on to the floor. Also, a couple of the tubes which ran from the kegs to the ceiling had been pulled down.

And on the floor, in the middle of this chaos, face-down, lay Warnock Belvedere.

Beside him was his walking stick. Ragged scrapings on its shiny surface suggested that it had been used to force the padlocks.

In Warnock's hand the bottle of Courvoisier was still clasped. It was empty. Beer from one of the broken plastic pipes bubbled fitfully over the thick tweed of his suit and into his stained beard.

God, the old soak must have been desperate. Finished the brandy bottle and still needed more. So he'd broken into the store-room, tried first to get some beer, and then attacked the spirits cupboard.

As Charles Paris looked down at the crumpled, sodden heap on the floor, and as his own head throbbed like an old dishwasher in its final cycle, he swore that he would never touch another drop.

Oh well, better wake the old bugger up, he thought. See if we're both going to be locked in here for the night.

He reached down to shake the prostrate actor's shoulder, but got no response.

He shook harder; then turned Warnock over on to his back.

The face revealed was grotesquely more purple and congested than usual.

Nobody was going to wake up Warnock Belvedere.

Ever again.

Chapter Eight

CHARLES TRIED THE Stage Door and the main doors in the Foyer. He tried the delivery door through which he had helped Norman with the beer kegs and he even tried the big shutter door of the scenery dock. They were all firmly locked from the outside.

He was imprisoned in the theatre with the corpse of Warnock Belvedere.

It gave him an uncomfortable feeling. He was unwilling to go back and look at the body, for in his imagination it had become more grotesque, the colour more livid, the eyes more bulging. Charles shuddered at the image. He felt ghastly. Apart from anything else, his head still seemed to be full of disgruntled piranha fish, nibbling away at it.

He would have to summon help. He went up to the administration area. The Artistic Director's door was locked, but fortunately Gavin's secretary had an extension line in the outer office. Charles picked it up. The dialling tone prompted him to wonder who he should ring.

Obviously the police. But maybe he should ring Gavin first. After all, the Pinero was Gavin's responsibility; he should be informed of the accident as soon as possible.

Yes, the director first, then the police.

Gavin lived alone. There had been a wife for some years, but because of his obsession with the theatre, she had rarely seen her husband. And when she finally walked out, Gavin had hardly noticed her absence.

The phone was answered on the third ring. Gavin sounded fully alert. Maybe he had been awake, agonizing over his production and how he was going to make up the lost rehearsal time. If that was the case, the news Charles was about to give wasn't going to ease his troubles.

"Gavin, it's Charles Paris. I'm calling from the theatre."

"Why the hell are you there?"

"I got locked in by mistake."

"And you want me to come and let you out?"

"Maybe, but in fact it's worse than that. Warnock Belvedere's here too."

"You and Warnock staying behind . . . well, there's a turn-up. What were—?"

Charles cut through this untimely attempt at humour. "Listen, Warnock's dead."

There was a silence from the other end of the phone. Then, in an appalled whisper, Gavin Scholes' voice said, "What, in my theatre?"

The police voice which answered the phone was impassive as it took down the details of what had happened. Or if the voice had any colouring at all, it was a tone of slight sceptical disbelief. Charles cursed all the alcohol he had had that night. He knew his speech was still slurred.

He explained that the theatre was locked, and gave them Gavin's address, so that the keys could be picked up. Yes, Mr Scholes would be awake; they had just spoken on the phone.

Right. The police would be along as soon as possible. Would Mr Paris please remain where he was until they arrived.

Fat bloody chance of doing anything else, he thought as he put the phone down.

The theatre was aggressively silent now, and it seemed full of the looming presence of Warnock Belvedere's body.

Charles shivered again. God, he felt terrible. Really needed a drink. As he walked down towards the foyer, he looked wistfully through the padlocked grille of Norman's bar.

For a moment, he thought of the open store-room downstairs. All those bottles. Or easy enough to fill a glass from the dribbling beer tubes . . .

81

But no. He didn't want to confront that congested face again.

Besides, he was going to give up the booze. Wasn't he?

The police were there in ten minutes, but it was a long ten minutes for Charles Paris. They came in through the Stage Door and he met them in the passage which led to the dressing rooms. There were two uniformed officers, but he could hear the sounds of other cars drawing up outside.

Charles felt very weary and unsteady. His words, he knew, were still fuzzy with drink, and he did not miss the sceptical exchange of looks between the two policemen as he showed them where Warnock Belvedere lay.

They thanked him politely and asked where they could find a telephone. They asked if he would mind waiting in the theatre for a while. In his dressing room? Yes, that would be fine. They wouldn't keep him longer than was necessary.

In the dressing room, Charles's head once again found the cushion of his table, and once again he dropped into a dead, unhealing sleep.

"Excuse me, sir. Mr Paris."

His shoulder was being shaken, and it took him a moment or two to realize where he was.

The policeman who was waking him was a new face. Not in uniform, this one. There was another unfamiliar figure in the doorway, and, beyond, he could see the anxious face of Gavin Scholes.

"Sorry," Charles mumbled through a mouthful of slimy cotton-wool. "Middle of the night, you know. Very tired."

"Yes, very tired, I'm sure, sir." Was he being hypersensitive to hear a hint of reproof in the policeman's voice? Oh, why on earth had he drunk so much?

"We don't want to keep you here longer than necessary this evening. But we would be most grateful if you could just describe exactly what happened."

82

"What, you mean when I found Warnock . . . the, er, body?"

"Well, yes, and before that. We've spoken to Mr Scholes about the earlier part of the evening. If you could take it from the moment that you left the bar at closing time . . . ?"

Suddenly the two policemen were sitting and one had a pencil poised over a notebook to take down Charles's words.

There didn't seem much to tell. Charles had spent most of the time between leaving the bar and discovering the body in an alcohol-induced stupor. How much detail did they want, he wondered. Did he have to tell them about peeing in the wash-basin? He decided to edit that detail out of his account.

"Why didn't the Stage Doorman realize that you were still in the theatre?"

"My dressing room light was not switched on."

"That seems rather strange. Why were you sitting in the dark?"

"Well, I just . . . I just didn't switch it on."

"I see." The words were delivered without emphasis, but their implication was apparent. The policeman turned to the door where Gavin still waited.

"Mr Scholes, would the Stage Doorman check that all the dressing rooms were empty?"

"He should do, yes."

"So, if he didn't, you're saying he was failing in his duties?"

No, that wasn't at all what Gavin wanted to say. His Stage Doorman had been at the Pinero for eleven years, and Gavin was very loyal to his staff. Somehow, these policemen had a way of making everything sound suspicious.

"Let's just say that on an evening like this the Stage Doorman might be more casual than when we've got a show on."

"I'm sorry. Could you explain that?"

"I mean that, while we're in rehearsal, there are fewer people around by the end of the evening. When there's a play actually in performance of course all the cast would be here till late, and

83

there'd still be a lot of members of the public in the bar and so on."

"Ah. I see. Thank you very much, Mr Scholes." The un-emotional tone was evenly maintained.

"Mr Paris, could you describe exactly what you saw when you went into the store-room? And, indeed, why you went in there in the first place?"

Charles explained about seeing the forced padlock, and described what he saw in the store-room. He knew he didn't do it very well. The words seemed too big for his mouth, and many of them got mixed up between his brain and his tongue.

At the end of his recitation, the policeman thanked him politely and asked for the address where he was staying.

"I don't think we need keep you any longer this evening, Mr Paris. I'm sure the best thing for you to do will be to go back to your digs and . . . sleep."

Again Charles wondered if he was unduly sensitive to that hesitation. Had the policeman really just stopped himself from saying, ". . . sleep it off"?

"Yes. Sure. Thank you." He rose gracelessly to his feet.

The policeman also rose and turned to Gavin. "I would like to talk to you a little more, Mr Scholes, about the late Mr Belvedere. If you don't mind . . . ? I realize it is very late."

"Oh, don't worry. I don't need much sleep. Anyway, once I've been woken up, that's it for the night. I never get back to sleep."

"Thank you, Mr Scholes. Shall we go up to your office?"

"Fine. See you in the morning, Charles."

"What, we'll be rehearsing as usual?"

"We must. Ten o'clock call, as ever. Somehow I've got to get this show on."

"What show is it you're rehearsing on at the moment, Mr Scholes?" the policeman asked politely.

"*Macbeth.*"

"Oh. That's the play that's meant to be bad luck, isn't it?"

"Yes," said Gavin wryly. "The Scottish Play." Then the

implication of Warnock's death struck him again. "Oh Christ, I'll have to get another Duncan." He looked hopefully at Charles who was walking past him with concentrated caution. "Charles, I wonder if you'd mind . . . ?"

"Sorry." A shake of the head. "Not that I don't want to help out, but I am the Bleeding Sergeant, aren't I? I think I'm as versatile as the next actor, but even I can't envisage standing up on stage and saying, 'What bloody man is that?' to myself."

"No. No," said Gavin wistfully. "Pity . . ."

The police kindly drove Charles back to his digs. When he got up to his room, and before he collapsed into the long-desired haven of bed, he looked through the curtains to the road outside.

The police car was still there.

A chill thought struck him.

Was the alcohol making him paranoid?

Or was he under surveillance?

Chapter Nine

THE NEXT MORNING the police car had gone, so Charles shrugged off his anxieties. Or at least he would have done, if shrugging hadn't been far too painful an activity for the delicately poised time-bomb which was now balanced on top of his neck. He had the worst hangover he could remember.

The gentle September light seemed to laser through his eyeballs into his brain. He took one look at his landlady's bacon, eggs and fried bread and had to leave the dining room, thus causing irremediable damage to their relationship—his landlady was one of those women whose emotional life is conducted solely through the medium of food and for whom every unconsumed crust or potato-skin is a mortal affront.

He couldn't face the claustrophobia of a bus, so he walked to the Pinero, arriving a little after ten. But the fresh air didn't help.

And what greeted him at the theatre did little to improve his mood. He was met at the Stage Door by the policeman of the night before who, courteous as ever, said, "Mr Paris, good morning. As I mentioned last night, I would like to talk to you a little further. Mr Scholes has kindly said that we may use his office, so if you'd care to come up with me straight away . . ."

"Oh yes. Fine. But I am meant to be rehearsing. Perhaps I'd better have a word with Gavin to—"

"That's quite all right, Mr Paris. I have spoken to Mr Scholes. I won't keep you any longer than necessary."

"Oh. All right."

They didn't speak again until they were up in Gavin's office. It was a crowded room, its every surface high with copies of *Spotlight*, scripts, set designs and the other impedimenta of theatre production.

The policeman sat at Gavin's desk and indicated a low chair for Charles. "Mr Scholes' secretary was kind enough to offer to make us coffee if we wanted any."

"It would be very welcome. Black, please."

"Of course."

The policeman, like a good host, went to the door and arranged the order. Then he returned to the chair. He looked very alert, in good condition for someone who had presumably been up most of the night.

"Sorry," said Charles. "I didn't get your name in all the confusion . . ."

"Detective Inspector Dowling."

"Ah."

The Detective Inspector looked up as someone entered the room. It wasn't the coffee. Instead, Charles was aware of the other plain-clothes policeman of the night before moving silently to take a chair in the corner behind him. "Detective Sergeant Halliwell will once again be taking notes. We have to have a record, obviously."

"Of course."

There was another pause while Gavin's secretary brought in the coffee. Charles gulped at his too avidly, burning his tongue.

When the door was safely closed behind the secretary, Detective Inspector Dowling, who had yet to touch his own coffee, looked directly at Charles. "Mr Paris, how well did you know Mr Belvedere?"

"I only met him about ten days ago, when we started rehearsal. Before that I'd heard a certain amount about him, but we'd never actually met."

"How had you heard about him?"

Charles shrugged. Incautiously. It still wasn't a good idea. His head felt as fragile as ever. "The theatre's a fairly small profession. You hear about people. Particularly the so-called 'characters'. Stories tend to build up about people who're 'larger than life'."

The Detective Inspector nodded. "And what had you heard about Mr Belvedere?"

"That he was an actor of the old school . . ."

"Could you clarify what that means for . . ." A helpless gesture of the hands ". . . a mere layman?"

"I suppose it means Warnock worked in a more flamboyant style than modern actors. More expansive . . . if you like, more hammy . . ." Charles caught the incomprehension on the Detective Inspector's face, ". . . likely to be a bit over-the-top . . ." That evidently wasn't much clearer, ". . . tended to overact a bit . . . ?"

"Ah. Thank you. I understand. And what else did you hear about him?"

"That he could be difficult."

"Difficult for whom in particular?"

"For a director. Actors of that generation don't really think directors are necessary, just kind of jumped-up Stage Managers. They think all the important bits of theatre come from the actors themselves."

"Thank you. This is fascinating, Mr Paris . . . you know, for me, coming into a place like this, knowing, I regret to say, very little about the theatre and theatrical people . . ." He paused, then changed his tone. This, Charles was beginning to recognize, was a technique with the Detective Inspector. First he would disarm with courtesy, then come in hard with the questions he really wanted to ask. "Would you say Mr Belvedere was liked amongst the group?"

It sounded wrong, the word "group". "Company" he should have said. But then, by his own admission, he knew nothing about the theatre.

Still, there was only one answer to the question. "No. He wasn't liked. I mean, some people were amused by him— he could be very funny, though usually in a pretty vicious way—but I would be lying if I said he was liked."

"Hmm." The Detective Inspector paused again. "Did you know that Mr Belvedere was homosexual?"

"Well, yes, obviously . . ." Charles shrugged again. Ooh, he must stop doing that. "But I mean, in the theatre, so many people are, you don't really think about it."

"No, I suppose not." For the first time, Charles caught a whiff of prejudice in the Detective Inspector's voice. For all his politeness and ingenuous enquiries, the man seemed to be building up a personal case against the theatre and theatrical people. Perhaps he was one of those who had always thought of actors as drunken, effeminate layabouts. If that were the case, what he had seen during the previous six hours would have done little to dispel the impression.

"I gather from Mr Scholes that Mr Belvedere was also a heavy drinker." The "also" suggested the Detective-Inspector was compiling a catalogue of the dead man's moral shortcomings.

"Yes."

"From the way he was found last night, one might assume that he had drunk a whole bottle of brandy."

"Yes."

"He also, I gather, had had a fair amount in the bar in the course of the day . . . ?"

"Yes."

"Surely that would be an excessive amount for him to drink?"

"Excessive, yes, but not out of character. I mean, he was notorious for going on benders."

"I gather quite a few actors do that . . ."

"Some." Charles found himself avoiding the Detective Inspector's eye.

"Do you think it possible that Mr Belvedere broke into that store-room in search of alcohol?"

"Well, one doesn't want to speak ill of the dead . . ."

"Much as I appreciate your delicacy, Mr Paris, I'm afraid we in the police sometimes have to ignore such niceties."

"Of course. Well, yes, then I would say it is possible. When I spoke to him before going into my dressing room last night, he did express an intention to get very drunk."

"Did he?" The Detective Inspector's head shook slightly in

disbelief at the existence of people who behaved like that. "Hmm, well, that would certainly conform with our findings so far. It'll have to be checked, but it seems fairly certain that Mr Belvedere's walking stick was the instrument used to force the padlocks on the door and cupboard."

"Ah."

There was another silence, before the next question was posed with studied casualness. "What do you think Mr Belvedere died of, Mr Paris?"

"I'm sorry?"

"Seems a straightforward question. What do you think killed him?"

"Well, I hadn't really thought." It was true. In the shock of discovering the body, and in the alcoholic haze in which he had discovered the body, Charles had not asked himself this basic question. "I don't know. I suppose, a heart attack . . . ? A stroke . . . ? He was grotesquely overweight. Or maybe just alcoholic poisoning . . . ?"

His interrogator shook his head. "None of those. He died of asphyxiation."

"You mean he was strangled?"

"No, no. We don't have to be so melodramatic, Mr Paris. Asphyxiation simply means the obstruction of the body's respiratory system. You don't have to strangle someone to achieve that. There are many other ways of cutting off the supply of air to the lungs."

"So what do you think happened in this case?"

"Well, we'll have to get it confirmed by forensic tests, but the police doctor's made a few educated guesses. I'll tell you what we think, because it's possible you might have some evidence to support our theories . . . you know, having been on the spot when it happened . . . albeit dead to the world at the time." This time there was no mistaking the edge of contempt in the Detective Inspector's look.

"Right, here's a scenario for what might have taken place. Mr Belvedere leaves the bar at closing time. He's had a lot to drink, but, being an alcoholic, he still wants more. He goes down to his dressing room and waits. You see him down there, but he presumably doesn't know that you stay in the building. He switches out the light in his dressing room, so that the Stage Doorman won't realize there's anyone there when he does his final rounds before locking up.

"When he's confident that the theatre's empty, Mr Belvedere, by now desperate for a drink, makes for the store-room. Using his walking-stick as a lever he forces open the door and then does the same to the lock of the cupboard. He steals a bottle of brandy and starts drinking it down, there on the spot. The brandy, on top of all the other alcohol he's had in the course of the day, makes him stagger around a bit, and that's when he pulls down the beer pipelines. Or maybe he just does that out of spite, or to make it look as though it's been an outside raid by kids . . . it's not really important which, the important thing is that the lines get broken.

"Then, finally, the alcohol gets to him, and he passes out, flat on the floor.

"Unfortunately, though, when the beer lines got broken, so too did the lines carrying gas to pump the beer. That gas, of course, is carbon dioxide, and an elementary knowledge of chemistry will tell you that it's heavier than air and so sinks to the ground. When it gets to the ground, it forces out the oxygen and so, for anyone who happens to be lying there, it's really rather bad news. Particularly in a room where there's a step up to the door, so that the gas stays trapped on the floor. Of course, someone in normal health would react, would rise to his feet when he started to have difficulty breathing. But for someone who was lying there in a drunken stupor . . ." The Detective Inspector shook his head ". . . I'm afraid it's going to be very bad news indeed."

"And that's what you think happened?" asked Charles.

"Seems a reasonable assumption. Subject to confirmation, as I say. See what comes out at the inquest. But yes, that's the way it looks at the moment."

"So you think it was an accident?"

Detective Inspector Dowling's eyes narrowed. "The only alternative to it being an accident, Mr Paris, would be murder."

"Yes."

The policeman sighed. "I know actors make their living by dramatizing things, but I don't think it's really necessary in this case. Looks like a straightforward accident to me. I don't think we need set in motion all the paraphernalia of a murder enquiry."

"Then why are you telling me all this?" Charles was, in part, relieved that the threat of his being a murder suspect had lifted, but he was also intrigued about the reasons for his interrogation.

"You were on the spot, Mr Paris. You may have seen something that invalidates my theory."

"Well, yes, I did, actually." Charles leapt in without thinking of the implication of his words.

"Oh yes?" The Detective Inspector was suddenly alert. Once again he had snapped from casual courtesy to incisive interrogation. "And what was that?"

"The brandy bottle."

"What about it?"

"Did you find a second brandy bottle?"

"No. Just the one."

"And you know it came from the store-cupboard?"

"We assume that."

"Because when I saw Warnock, before the store-room had been broken into, he already had a bottle of Courvoisier."

"Are you sure of that, Mr Paris?"

"Well, yes, I . . . ." But suddenly he wasn't sure of anything. The night before was disappearing into a jumble of alcoholic images. "I'm fairly sure."

"Fairly, eh?" Detective Inspector Dowling grimaced. "We in the police force prefer things to be a bit firmer than 'fairly', you know. But let's say for a moment you're right. . . . What you're suggesting is that someone set up the whole thing, got Mr Belvedere drunk, broke into the store-room, laid him on the floor, fractured the beer- and gas-lines . . . all getting pretty elaborate, isn't it, Mr Paris?"

"Yes, I agree, but—"

"And then of course if you are talking in those terms, it raises the question of *who*, doesn't it? Who are you suggesting set up this complicated scenario?"

"Well . . ."

"Mr Paris, if you'll pardon my saying it, you are not what the police regard as an ideal witness. During the period of what you like to think of as the murder, you were, not to put too fine a point on it, incapable with drink. I've spoken to other people who were in the bar with you last night . . . apparently you couldn't even stand up when you left. So I think anything you say about your encounter with the late Mr Belvedere must be a little suspect, don't you . . . ?"

"I'm sure he had a bottle then. He said that a generous friend had given it—"

"There is another point, too, Mr Paris, which I'm sure you will in time work out for yourself . . ."

"What's that?"

"If we are talking about a murder, so far as we know there was only one other person in the theatre at the time that Mr Belvedere died. Wasn't there, Mr Paris?"

The implications of Detective Inspector Dowling's words sunk in, as Charles went down to join the rehearsal.

He just didn't know. The policeman's manner was so deceptive. Maybe he genuinely did think that the death had been accidental. Or maybe that was just a ploy to disorient Charles, to put him off his guard.

One thing was clear, though. If the police were thinking in terms of murder, they had only one suspect.

And that was Charles Paris.

Chapter Ten

"YOU'RE NO FUN any more, Charles Paris," said John B. Murgatroyd, slurping a lunchtime pint in the bar.

Charles squinted down at his Perrier water. "No."

"I mean, what you need is a hair of the dog."

"That's what I had yesterday. I had so many hairs of the dog I could have knitted myself my own St. Bernard. And it didn't do me any good."

"No. But that was yesterday. Today's today."

"I know. I'm still laying off."

"But, after the shock of discovering old Warnock's body, you need *something*."

"That's true."

"What'll it be?"

"I'll stick with this." He looked again at the Perrier water. It didn't get any less pallid and uninspiring. Had he been a vodka drinker, or a gin drinker, perhaps it wouldn't have looked so strange. But to a man whose familiar spectrum of beverages ranged only from the gold of Bell's whisky to the russet of bitter, there was a mental jolt each time he looked at it.

John B. shook his head in mixed pity and disbelief. "Sad to see a good man go."

"Sad to see Warnock go . . . ?" Charles ventured.

"Well, yes. Sad to see anyone go, obviously. But I don't think the old bastard's going to be mourned that much."

"No."

"Couldn't be a more appropriate end, though, could it? Drowned in alcohol."

"That isn't quite what happened."

94

"Well, to all intents and purposes. I mean, it was the booze that got him . . . or at least, the desire for the booze."

"Yes."

Something in Charles's tone made John B. look at him sharply. "Oh, I understand. That's it. Seeing him lying there's put you off."

"I suppose so. I mean, I've heard the expression 'old soak' enough times, but I never thought I'd see it so literally demonstrated. The beer was just dribbling over him. His suit was like a wet dishcloth."

"Yuk. Still, a few people round the theatre won't be sorry."

"Who were you thinking of in particular?" asked Charles, suddenly alert.

"You name them. Little Ms. RSC, certainly. Now perhaps she'll get a Duncan who will allow her to . . ." John B. dropped into a parody of her thrilling intensity ". . . *concentrate on the subtext of her part.*"

"Hmm."

"I've come to the conclusion that what would sort her out is a really thorough screwing. By an expert."

"Are you volunteering or just giving your considered medical opinion?"

"Bit of each."

"Well, good luck. I'll know when you've succeeded by your bent ears. Incidentally, Doctor, could I just ask why it is that you always recommend the same treatment for every female complaint?"

John B. dropped instantly into a cod Viennese accent. "In my experience, Herr Paris, it seems to work wiz most of them."

"You are a sexist pig and I shouldn't be listening to you."

"Please yourself."

"Who else, though?"

"Who else what?"

"Who else do you think will be glad to see the back of Warnock?"

"Well, everything Felicia does and thinks, someone else does and thinks, doesn't he?"

"Yes," said Charles ruminatively, remembering the embarrassments of the first evening when Warnock Belvedere had made a pass at Russ Lavery.

"And dear old Gavin was having enough disciplinary problems without Warnock constantly undermining his authority."

"True."

"But, as I said, basically anyone in the company. One of the most popular deaths in the annals of the theatre, I'd say. A blessed accident."

Charles didn't question this. No one in the company seemed to have thought of any possibility other than accident. Again he wondered how much Detective Inspector Dowling believed that conclusion, or how much he was playing his chief suspect along. Giving him enough rope . . .

"Come on, let me get you another drink, Charles. What's it to be? You can't pretend you're enjoying that Perrier."

"No."

"Go on, have a pint."

"No, I won't."

"A Bell's?"

"No. I am really on the wagon."

"Dear oh dear. Well, what then—Coke, grapefruit juice, lemonade, cherryade, Tizer . . . ?" John B. pronounced each name with mounting distaste.

"All of those are so bloody sweet, that's the trouble."

"I know the solution," said John B. triumphantly. "I bet Norman's got one of those alcohol-free lagers tucked away somewhere."

Charles raised a hand of restraint. "No. I may have few principles, but the idea of alcohol-free lager offends one of my deepest. It's like . . . yuk, I don't know . . . like the idea of making love to an inflatable woman."

John B. chuckled. "See, there's nothing else you like. You're going to have to have a proper drink."

96

"No," said Charles resolutely.

"If you don't, I am going to leave you on your own and start my campaign to winkle my way into Felicia Chatterton's knickers."

"Off you go then. Good luck. I'm going to stick to my Perrier."

"Sissy." John B. started to move away.

"Just a minute." Charles gestured his friend close and whispered, "I think your best approach is to find a subtext that proves Lady Macbeth was having an affair with Lennox. Then she'll leap into bed with you, no problem . . . you know, Stanislavsky, 'Method', all that . . ."

"Hey, thanks. That's a brilliant idea. You can't think of any particular lines of Lennox's that'd be suitable, can you?"

"'Fraid not. There doesn't seem to be a moment where he suddenly says, 'How about it then, Lady Macbeth? Get 'em off'."

"No." For a moment John B. looked downcast. Then inspiration struck. He raised a finger in triumph. "I've got it. I'll tell her those lines were in the original text, but they got cut from the First Folio. Can't fail. See you, Charles."

When John B. Murgatroyd had sauntered off, Charles was left once again with his own thoughts. And they weren't very comforting ones.

Also he did very desperately miss having a drink. Usually the worst effects of a hangover could be temporarily suspended by a lunchtime top-up, but his vow had forbidden that option. He thought back to the old joke about a drunkard having the advantage over a teetotaller that he knew from the moment he woke up, his day could only get better. What faced Charles was a long plateau of boredom.

But he was determined to stick with it. Enough people had told him over the years to lay off the booze. How gratified they would all be to know that he was finally taking their advice.

Frances, in particular. She'd be glad. From the start of their marriage, she'd been on at him, subtly but inexorably, to cut down. And now he was doing it.

That might be a good way of making contact again . . . Ring her and tell her he was on the wagon. He could offer his great sacrifice as a peace-offering.

Good idea, yes. He could go straight away and ring her at school. She was usually free to take phone-calls at lunchtime.

But he curbed his enthusiasm. It remained a good idea, but it would probably be even better if he waited a few days. Frances might not think giving up drink for fourteen hours was really worth crowing about. But when it got to fourteen days, yes, then it could be a useful re-opening gambit.

It didn't take long for his thoughts to move from his magnificent self-denial back to Warnock Belvedere's death.

He'd really got himself into a cleft stick over that. If he accepted Detective Inspector Dowling's view of the death as an accident, then he had to deny certain memories he had of the night before. He knew he had been pretty fuddled, but he was sure that Warnock had had a bottle of Courvoisier before the store-room was forced, and also that the old actor had said it was the gift of "a generous friend".

But if he continued to maintain that memory, the only effect would be to concentrate the Detective Inspector's suspicions on him. Better, in that sense, to let sleeping dogs—or asphyxiated old queens—lie.

On the other hand, if Dowling was simply trying to put him off his guard, then he was still in danger. Any allegation of murder immediately pointed the finger at him as the murderer. So far as the police knew, he was the only person who had had the opportunity. The means were easily organized and, as for motive, well, everyone hated Warnock. He was sure members of the company could recall insults directed at Charles Paris as much as at anyone else.

So, in a sense, the only way he could protect himself against a charge of murder was by proving that someone else had committed it.

Because, however much he fudged round the issue, Charles Paris kept coming back to the certainty that Warnock Belvedere had been murdered.

It wasn't just the brandy bottle which he was now certain he had seen in the old actor's hand while the store-room door was still intact. There were a couple of other details.

First, there was Warnock's mention of "a generous friend". That implied that someone had given him the bottle, secure in the knowledge that the actor was likely to swig away until it was empty.

But more significant was another fact, which Charles had omitted, by genuine oversight, to mention to the police. Now, not wishing to encourage them towards suspicions of murder, he was quite glad of that oversight.

The second important fact was that when he went into the store-room, the light had been off. If Warnock Belvedere had followed the course of action which Detective Sergeant Dowling described, there was no way that he would have done it in the dark.

Which meant that someone else had switched the light off.

The show, as theatrical cliché and the economic health of the Pinero Theatre, Warminster, demanded, had to go on. Warnock Belvedere had been quickly replaced. One phone-call from Gavin had procured an elderly actor of benign competence contracted to start rehearsal on the Wednesday morning. No extravagant, inventive casting this time. The director had gone for someone who lived locally and with whom he had worked many times before. Given only two weeks to the opening night, he opted for safety. And there was a general relieved feeling in the cast that the production would be more relaxed without the flamboyant malignancy of Warnock Belvedere.

As it had on Charles (though in his case more literally), the death had had a sobering effect on the whole company. They had all felt slightly guilty about the lack of discipline which had been creeping into rehearsals, and slightly schoolboyish over the way they had taken advantage of Gavin's weakness. Warnock's demise had been a well-timed slap on the wrist, and they all settled down with renewed concentration to make sure that *Macbeth* would be ready in time for the paying public to enjoy.

It was just as well that they were prepared to work hard, because there was a long way to go. Apart from the problems of integrating a new Duncan and a new Macduff's Son into the production, there was also the problem of George Birkitt. His sojourn in Paris seemed to have wiped from his mind all trace of the previous week's rehearsal, and certainly very few of Shakespeare's lines appeared to have taken any lasting hold on the slippery surface of his memory. For him, the Tuesday rehearsal was like starting again at Day One.

Felicia Chatterton's concentration, of course, could not be faulted, but at times Gavin Scholes wished it could have been differently channelled. Since her approach to acting required that every intonation and movement should "feel right", rehearsal was frequently interrupted by long silences while she tried to make the mental adjustment that one of Gavin's instructions necessitated.

On the Tuesday afternoon, for example, they were working on the Sleepwalking Scene. Felicia's neurotic trauma was very convincing; Charles could feel the power of her talent whenever he was on stage with her.

"'To bed, to bed; there's knocking at the gate,'" she intoned in a tinglingly agonized whisper. "'Come, come, come, come, give me your hand. What's done—'"

"Erm, can I just stop you there . . . ?" Gavin, who was leaning against the front of the stage, interposed.

"Sorry?" She seemed to come out of a trance. "Yes . . . ?"

"I think we want to make that a bit sexier, Felicia."

"Sexier?"

"Yes. It's a hark back to the strong physical thing between the Macbeths we got going in Act One."

"Oh, do you think so?"

"Yes." Gavin didn't sound quite so sure now, but hoped he might convince her with a textual argument. "It's in the words, love. 'To bed' . . . 'come'. It's definitely sexual imagery."

"Hmm." Felicia gave this studied consideration. "I suppose it might be. Certainly 'to bed' has a sexual resonance . . ."

"Yes," Gavin agreed eagerly.

"But I'm not sure about 'come'. I've a feeling its sexual connotation is more recent. Nineteenth century, I think. I mean, we know that 'die' meant 'achieve orgasm' in Shakespeare's time, but I'm not sure about 'come'. Maybe we could look it up . . . ?"

"Well, yes . . ." Gavin was beginning to regret having started up this particular avenue. "I mean, I'm not so concerned about the actual words . . ."

"Aren't you?" asked Felicia, shocked.

"Well, yes, of course I *am*. I am. But I mean, it's more a *feeling* that I want to come across."

"Ye-es?" She sounded uncertain.

"You see, we've established at the beginning of the play that the Macbeths have this strong sexual thing . . ."

"Yes."

"And that a good part of her power over him is based on what she can do for him in bed . . ."

"Sure."

"And then, when he starts to get real power—i.e. when he becomes king—her sexual power over him is weaker. He goes his own way, he starts to exclude her from his plans . . ."

She nodded her earnest blond head. "'Be innocent of the knowledge, dearest chuck.'"

"Exactly. So really that signals the beginning of the breakdown of the marriage. He doesn't need her any more. He thinks he can manage on his own now he's got power. The balance of the relationship has shifted . . ."

"Yes. I accept that."

"Probably the balance of the sexual relationship has shifted too. Maybe he is now the initiator. Unfortunately, we can't be sure . . ." Gavin lightened the atmosphere with a little joke. "Shakespeare didn't write any bedroom scenes for the Macbeths."

"No," Felicia concurred with unfeigned regret. "It's a pity, isn't it?"

"Yes, anyway, what I'm saying is that the sleepwalking scene expresses the breakdown of Lady Macbeth's personality under the stresses of what she's done, and I think it also expresses the breakdown of her marriage—i.e. her sexuality—and I think we want an echo of that, a reminder of what the sexual relationship used to be like—in this scene."

"Hmm . . ."

"I mean, as well as everything else, as well as her revulsion for the monster she has unleashed in her husband . . ."

"Hmm . . ." Felicia Chatterton's pretty little brow wrinkled as she endeavoured to accommodate this new idea.

"You see," Gavin went on, "I think this scene's got to be sexy. We can help it with the cozzy. I mean, I think the nightgown's got to be really low-cut, show us a lot of . . . you know. In a way, I think that makes it more poignant. I mean, it's one of the reasons I wanted to cast a young Lady Macbeth . . . so that what we witness is not some menopausal breakdown but the crack-up of a woman at her physical peak."

"Yes. And you think I can get all that into the 'to bed' lines?"

"Well, I hoped so. But if you think it's too difficult . . ."

"No, no, no." She brought her hand up to her face and held the bridge of her nose between thumb and finger as she focused her concentration on the problem. "Just give me a minute to see how I can make it work."

The minute of silence stretched to two minutes. Charles, in his role of the Scottish Doctor, shuffled his feet and tried to avoid the eye of the Waiting-Gentlewoman, in case he giggled.

Felicia Chatterton remained immobile, shoehorning the new thought into her mind and seeing how it fitted.

"Erm . . ." said Gavin eventually. "I think we'd better move on."

"Yes, sure, I know, Gavin, but what you've just suggested is a kind of re-interpretation of the whole part . . . I mean, a shift in her relationship with everything around her."

"Yes, I take that."

"Going to take a bit of time to work out the ramifications . . ."

"Yes," Gavin agreed, bitterly regretting that he'd ever given the note. "Well, if you could possibly just, sort of, work out the ramifications later, you know, in your own time, and if you could just, for the minute, say the lines a bit sexier . . . ?"

"What, without working out *why* I'm saying them sexier?"

"Exactly." The director looked jubilant. She had got his point at last.

"Well . . ." said Felicia Chatterton dubiously. "I suppose I could *try* . . ."

All of this, inevitably, took time. And, unfortunately for Charles, he was not occupied during that time. He was standing on stage, true, but he didn't have a lot to do—just deliver the occasional line in the intervals between Lady Macbeth's agonizing over her motivations. As a result, his mind was free to wander. And it kept wandering back to the same predictable subject.

If Warnock Belvedere had been murdered, the main suspects for that murder were the people who had been in the bar at the end of the Monday evening, when Charles had made his ignominious exit. He strained his memory to recall the scene. It hurt his head to concentrate. His brain felt bruised and dry, unaided by the temporary assistance of a lunchtime drink.

Who had been there? Norman, behind the bar. His wife, Sandra, as ever ignoring him, on the other side of the counter. Felicia Chatterton and Russ Lavery, rapt over more open-heart surgery on the character of Lady Macbeth. Gavin Scholes, with Lady Macduff and two Witches.

Given Warnock Belvedere's propensity for putting everyone's back up, any one of them might have had a motive for wanting him out of the way.

Hmm, Charles thought without enthusiasm, I'm going to have to start checking on the movements of all of them, aren't I?

Chapter Eleven

LADY MACDUFF AND the two Witches were quickly eliminated.

Charles didn't have to be overelaborate in his enquiries. An apology for his drunkenness and the confession that he couldn't remember anything of the previous evening got Lady Macduff talking, with suitably theatrical emphases, about how *ghastly* it had been for Warnock to have died like that, and how *awful* to feel that if only they'd stayed in the theatre a little longer they might have been able to *help*.

"Why, what time did you leave?" Charles asked casually.

"Almost immediately after you did. Gavin gave us a lift. Our house is on his way home."

The three actresses, it transpired, were sharing a rented house some four miles from the theatre. Gavin had deposited them there together at about half past eleven. So, unless he wanted to get into elaborate conspiracy theories or imagine them walking back and breaking into the theatre, Charles could rule Lady Macduff and the two Witches out of his investigations.

Mind you, he thought, if I open the enquiry up to people who could have broken into the theatre . . . or indeed people who might have hidden themselves in the theatre all evening and not gone up to the bar, the field becomes infinitely wide. At least I'll start with the obvious ones.

He didn't rule out Gavin Scholes along with the actresses whom he had driven home. The director stayed on the list. For a start, he had suffered publicly from Warnock Belvedere's attacks on his professional competence, which gave him a degree of motive. Also, he had a car, which made returning five miles to the theatre no problem. And, most significantly, he had keys which would let him into the theatre once he got there. What was more, he knew the building so well that he could easily have worked out the potential of the liquor store-room as a scene for a murder.

But there was another person on the theatre staff who knew that store-room even better.

Norman Phipps wasn't in the bar at the end of the Tuesday's rehearsals, so Charles prepared to give his order to a spotty youth in a bow-tie.

He had to bite back his instinctive, "Large Bell's, please." He was really determined about this not drinking business. His body and his soul both needed the scouring of abstinence.

But actually thinking of what to order again presented a problem. Perrier still seemed too insipid; he wanted something with a bit of taste.

"Um, could I have a . . . ?"

"Yes?" prompted the spotty youth, aware of the increasing arrivals of actors at the end of rehearsal. Charles, even off the booze, had not lost his practised skill at being first to the bar.

"Um, a, er . . ."

"What? Come on, I've got lots of people to serve."

"Yes. A . . . er . . ." He took the plunge. "Tonic water."

"Ice and lemon?" the barman asked as he turned to the shelf of bottles.

"What's the alternative?"

The spotty face looked back balefully. "No ice and lemon."

"That's all you can have with tonic water, is it?"

"Some people," the spotty youth replied in a voice heavy with long-suffering, "have gin or vodka with it."

"No, I meant non-alcoholic."

"Ice and lemon is the most usual. Angostura bitters some people ask for." This was spoken with undisguised contempt.

"Oh, get on with it," urged a thirsty Donalbain, pressing against the counter.

"I'll try the Angostura," Charles concluded hastily.

It wasn't very nice. As he sipped it, he reflected that he'd never liked pink gin much. And pink tonic water excluded the only element that made pink gin even mildly tolerable. Also it was bloody expensive. The prices of soft drinks were iniquitous. For the first time in his life he felt the righteous anger of the teetotaller against the discrimination of an alcohol-oriented world.

He looked across the bar-room to John B. Murgatroyd steering two fistfuls of pints to a seated group of actors. Oh dear, was giving up the booze going to lose him friends as well?

He wondered where Norman was. Obviously the Bar Manager couldn't be expected always to be on duty, but he had been behind the counter for most of the previous week. Saving money on staff, no doubt. After all, with just the cast rehearsing, business was fairly slack. He'd need to draft in extra help once the season really started with the opening of *Macbeth*.

But, even as he thought this, the next best thing to Norman entered the bar. Sandra Phipps was, as ever, dressed to emphasize her sexuality, this time in a tight flying-suit of shiny scarlet material. Perhaps a bit too tight. The constricting belt drew attention to the little roll of fat at her waist, a legacy presumably of bearing Stewart.

Charles waved to her and she came across to him readily enough. "Get you a drink?" he asked.

"Ooh, you men," she simpered. "Always trying to get girls drunk, aren't you?"

He began to wonder if there was any question in the world to which Sandra Phipps would not give a sexually loaded answer.

Still, he played along. "Of course," he leered. "You know we're only after one thing."

She giggled and said thank you, yes, she'd like a Tia Maria. Somehow, that seemed to him to epitomize her character, cloyingly sweet and in some way synthetic.

He gave the spotty youth the order. "And I'll have a . . ."

"What?"

"Um . . ."

"How was the tonic and Angostura?"

"Quite revolting."

The spotty youth nodded. "Could have told you that."

"Well, is there anything you could tell me that is nice?"

"Lot of things. Bell's whisky's not bad."

"I know that," Charles said testily. "I mean, non-alcoholic things."

"No. You got me there." He addressed his mind to the problem. "I have seen people," he offered cautiously, "drinking alcohol-free lager . . ."

"Does it make them look happy?"

The spotty youth shook his head. "Miserable as sin."

Charles threw in the towel. "Oh, I'll have a tomato juice."

"Worcester sauce?"

"Yes. Salt. Pepper. Eggs. Ketchup. Everything you've got."

"Vodka?"

Ooh, it was tempting. His head still felt as if it had been the match ball in a South American Cup Final. And surely a Bloody Mary was just medicinal . . .

But virtue triumphed. "No, thank you."

After all, it was going to be his peace offering to Frances. A dried-out husband. Goodness, she'd think her birthday and Christmas had both come at once. Must ring Frances, he thought. Must ring Frances.

He took the drinks across to where Sandra perched on a bar-stool, stroking her scarlet thighs.

"Cheers."

She raised her glass. "May you always get enough."

Predictable again.

"Norman not about?" he asked casually, thinking how he could ease the conversation round to the questions he wanted to ask.

But her reply removed that necessity. "He's with the police."

"Oh?"

She giggled. He was aware that, beneath her customary

brassiness, she was very nervous. "Yes. Do you reckon they'll 've arrested him yet?"

"What for?"

"The murder of Warnock Belvedere."

"What? Goodness, it never occurred to me that the old queen might have been murdered," Charles lied.

"No, of course he wasn't." She giggled. "Only joking."

"So why do the police want to see Norman?"

"Check out about how he kept the store-room. He was quite worried going to see them."

"Why?"

"Well, he's the licensee here, isn't he? If they can prove negligence, you know, if there was something wrong down in the store-room, he'd be liable. Big insurance claim is the last thing he needs."

"Yes. I've had a couple of sessions with the police," Charles confided, softening her up before he started on the important questions.

"Oh yes. Why?"

"Well, I found the body."

"Of course. How did they treat you?"

"I think they're deeply suspicious of me."

"Why?"

"My behaviour last night was a bit . . . well . . ."

"Yes, you were well gone." She paused, then probed, "What did the police seem to think?"

"About Warnock's death?"

"Yes."

"That it was an accident."

"That's a relief." She relaxed for a moment before a new thought struck her. "Unless, as I say, they reckon Norman's responsible for that accident."

"They didn't imply that. They seem to reckon Warnock just broke into the store-room and was so pissed he tore all the pipes down. I don't think any of the joints were loose or anything."

"Good." She looked at Charles as if he had somehow

demanded an explanation. "Like I say, big insurance claim we could really do without. Always bloody hard-up. Why I didn't pick a husband who was going to make a few bob I don't know. And now we've got Stewart's school fees to find . . ."

"How's Stewart taking it, being out of the play? Is he very upset?"

"He'll survive," Sandra Phipps replied briskly, putting an end to the subject.

"Have you had to talk to the police . . . ?" Charles ventured.

"Yes. I think they're working through everyone who was in the bar last night."

Just as I am, he thought. Oh, the pointlessness of being an amateur sleuth, always limping a few steps behind the professionals. No doubt Detective Inspector Dowling and his acolytes already knew everything. They knew the death had been murder and they knew who had done it.

That made him feel uncomfortable. He still felt exposed as a potential suspect. He took a swig from his drink, but tomato juice didn't soothe him the way whisky would have done.

Once again, he came back to the conclusion that to clear his name he must pursue his own investigations. "So did the police ask when you left the bar last night?"

"Oh yes."

"And when Norman left?"

She looked at him suspiciously. "You're as bad as they are. Everyone's so bloody suspicious."

He tried to shift her mood with a platitude. "I'm afraid that's what happens when something like a murder occurs."

"Yes. Yes. Suppose you're right."

"And I suppose you were able to put their minds at rest . . . ?"

Again she looked up sharply. "Yes, I was. Norman and I left together. Soon as he'd locked up the bar."

"You drove home?"

"We walked. Only live the other side of the park. Always walk when we're both going to leave at the same time. If I'm going to be on my own I take the car. Nasty types around that park."

"Yes. Oh well, at least you were able to put Detective Inspector Dowling's mind at rest."

"Oh, sure. Mind you, he's a nosy bugger."

"What do you mean?"

"Well, it wasn't just when did we leave. It was when did we get home, what did we do when we got home. Did we both stay at home all night?"

"I suppose that's because you live so near the theatre . . ."

"You mean they reckon one of us could have nipped back in the middle of the night?"

Charles shrugged. Even so far into his hangover, he was reminded that shrugging was a bad idea. "Presumably they have to check everything."

"Yes, well, fortunately . . ." Sandra Phipps leant close. Charles could smell the pungency of her musky perfume. "I was able to give them chapter and verse. Embarrassing, isn't it, to have to describe your sex-life to the police?"

"Oh," said Charles, mildly embarrassed himself.

"Thing is," she went on coarsely, "when Norman wants a bit, he really wants a bit. Amazing I ever get any sleep. At it till three o'clock last night he was." There was a note of reluctant pride in her voice.

Charles felt a little shocked. He had got used to Sandra loading her every remark with sexual innuendo, but to hear her talking so glibly about the real thing was unsettling. It also put a whole new light on to her relationship with Norman. However much she diminished and dismissed him in public, it was clear from her words that he was the dominant partner in their sexual relationship. Once again, Charles was brought up against the immovable fact that it is impossible to see inside another couple's marriage.

"Ah," he said. This didn't really seem an adequate reaction to what she had just said, but he couldn't think of anything else.

Sandra laughed raucously. "As I say, dead embarrassing to

have to tell that kind of thing to the police." But she didn't sound embarrassed. She enjoyed talking about it, particularly, Charles realized, to strangers. He was being used, just as the police had been, to give her some kind of thrill.

"Anyway," she concluded, "at least that let us off the hook as far as any police enquiries go."

As she spoke, she looked up and a flicker of anxiety crossed her face. Norman was walking towards her.

He nodded to Charles. "No problem," he said quietly to his wife.

"They're not worried about negligence?"

Norman Phipps paused almost imperceptibly, then shook his head. "No, they reckon everything was secure. Anything that was done, Warnock Belvedere did to himself."

Sandra looked relieved. She had been genuinely worried about the threat to their livelihood.

Without further words, Norman went across to the bar to relieve the spotty youth. Charles couldn't help his eyes from following the Bar Manager, fascinated by this new dimension, this new identity of Norman Phipps, Superstud.

But at least, he reflected, that rules out both of the Phippses. If they left the bar together at half-past eleven, and were then erotically engaged till three in the morning, there was no way that either of them could have arranged the death of Warnock Belvedere.

Chapter Twelve

ON THE WEDNESDAY of the second week's rehearsal, the new
Duncan was quickly integrated into the production. It was a
painless process. He was a quick-learning old pro and, though
he lacked the stage presence of his late predecessor in the role,
he also lacked Warnock's other, less endearing qualities, and no
one in the company regretted the exchange.

The whole of the Thursday was spent on Act Five, which
involved almost everyone. To swell the battle scenes, Gavin had
enlisted even the three Witches and Lady Macduff, who he
hoped, under sufficiently large helmets, would pass for
members of Macbeth's or Malcolm's armies. Since the new
Duncan did not share Warnock Belvedere's fastidiousness
about doubling, he was also conscripted.

In fact, the only members of the company who would not be
disguising themselves as Birnham Wood or dashing around the
theatre with strange battle-cries were Macduff's Son and Lady
Macbeth. This was just as well for the sake of the former's
schooling and the sake of the latter's stamina.

The intensity which Felicia Chatterton put into her acting
was beginning to take its toll. She looked exhausted when she
came in to the Wednesday's rehearsal, her wonderful blue eyes
smudged around with tiredness, and she kept stretching as if
she were in pain from her back. Charles wondered whether the
problem was one of pacing, if she was trying to cram into
three-and-a-half weeks' rehearsal the mental processes of five or
six weeks'.

She also seemed to have distanced herself from her confidant,
Russ Lavery. It had been noticeable on the Tuesday that they
did not sit together in the auditorium during rehearsal, and that
they did not eat together upstairs in the bar at lunchtime.

Charles wondered what had happened between them. The obvious cause of the estrangement—or the one that he would find most obvious—was that Russ had finally had enough of Felicia's wittering on and was taking a rest. But that didn't fit in with the doleful expression on his face or the way his eyes followed her every movement. There seemed to have been some actual rift, and Felicia seemed to have been its initiator.

Charles decided he must try to find out what had happened. After all, both Russ and Felicia had been in the bar on the Monday evening. Both were therefore potential suspects for Warnock Belvedere's murder.

So on the Thursday, while Felicia was, it was hoped, having a much-needed rest, Charles determined that he would get a private word with Russ Lavery.

It was easier to make the determination than to achieve it. The battle scenes proved to be very demanding, and the entire cast was kept rushing round the theatre, with little opportunity for casual conversation, let alone pertinent interrogation.

Gavin's approach to the battles was as traditional as his approach to the Apparition Scene and the rest of the play. Rather than recognizing the numerical limitations of his cast and opting for some form of stylized action, he went determinedly for spectacle. He wanted to fill the stage with soldiers, to vie with the splendours of Hollywood in his presentation of warfare.

This, though an admirable intention, was difficult to achieve with two armies which, even allowing for the conscription of Lady Macduff and the Witches, not to mention sudden changes of allegiance by Charles Paris, still only totalled sixteen.

"Don't worry," Gavin kept saying, "we'll fill the stage with soldiers."

The company, all trying to take up as much space as possible, looked at the large areas of emptiness around them, and could perhaps be forgiven for doubting their director's word.

"It'll be all right," Gavin went on. "It's there in the text, after all. They cut down the branches of Birnham Wood to 'shadow the numbers of their host', so that the enemy can't count precisely how many there are. They just give an impression of great numbers. That's exactly what we'll do."

"But," John B. Murgatroyd, who was holding up a mop (a rehearsal prop to represent a Birnham branch) objected, "what happens when we our 'leavy screens throw down, and show like those we are'? Isn't there a bit of a danger the audience might laugh?"

"I don't see why. I mean, we're not pretending you're the whole army. Just a sort of vanguard, you know, with the leaders up the front."

"Well, how did we get cut off from the rest of the army?" John B. persisted. "And aren't we going to be a bit exposed if Macbeth sends his army out after us?"

"Hmm . . ." Gavin looked pensive.

"Anyway, whoever heard of an army whose leaders were at the front?"

"Well, what are you suggesting as an alternative, John B.?" asked Gavin, seduced into the notion that the actor was raising serious points about his production.

"Suppose we kept on carrying our 'leavy screens' right to the end . . . ? Then the audience still wouldn't be able to count us."

"Ye-es . . . but then we'd have to cut the lines about throwing down the 'leavy screens'. The Schools Matinees wouldn't like that."

"But it'd help Macbeth's motivation if we kept the branches. Then it would seem as if Birnham Wood was still marching towards him."

For a moment Gavin accepted the logic of this. Then he saw the objection. "But how could you fight if you were still holding your bits of wood?"

"We could hit the enemy with them," suggested John B., who was beginning to have difficulty controlling the tremor of laughter in his voice.

"Hmm . . ."

"And we could have a new battle cry." The actor brandished

his mop as he shouted, "'Join Malcolm's Army! It's the best! We have branches everywhere!'"

This line, and the company laughter that attended it, finally made the director realize that he was being sent up. So he had a little tantrum and bawled John B. Murgatroyd out.

But it was the only breakdown of discipline in a hard-working day. And, whether the cast thought Gavin's method of presenting the battle-scenes was effective or not, by the end of rehearsal they all knew exactly the effects he wanted and how they were to be achieved.

By six o'clock Charles Paris felt physically very tired. For a man in his fifties, whose only gesture towards keeping fit was occasionally watching athletics on television, all that rushing up and down stairs, round the back of the stage and through the auditorium had taken its toll.

He felt in anguished need of a restorative pint or two. But he restrained himself. He was determined to stick with the new regime. Till . . . Till when . . . ? He didn't know, but in a strange way his abstinence had become tied in with the murder. He wouldn't have a drink until he knew who had killed Warnock Belvedere.

Good heavens, now he really *did* have an incentive to solve the case.

Maybe, he thought, my brain will work better unfogged by alcohol. But there didn't seem much evidence of it. His mind still circled round the same handful of fixed facts, without making those intuitive leaps which he hoped for. Maybe, he thought cynically, it's all nonsense about such stimulants slowing you down. Perhaps I should go the whole hog, like Sherlock Holmes, and take up cocaine?

He ran through the possible advantages that not drinking gave him. His pledge was now sixty-seven hours old, and it was time for an assessment.

Well, for a start he hadn't got a hangover . . .

Second, he was sleeping better. On both the Tuesday and the

Wednesday nights he had slept deeply, not even having to get up for his customary three-thirty pee.

And then . . . Well, presumably he was saving money.

And he was probably helping his long-term health prospects.

And, um . . .

No, that seemed to be all the advantages.

What was there to be said on the other side?

Well, he missed it desperately. Not in an agonized, physical way—he really didn't think he was chemically dependent—but he just missed the reassurance of a glass in his hand and the comforting warmth of whisky burning down his throat.

He also missed the punctuation of his day. For almost all his life he been attuned to the soothing diurnal rhythms of opening times and closing times. Without them he felt disoriented and dispossessed.

He missed the conviviality of getting drunk at the same pace as other people. He missed the communal element of drinking. In fact, not drinking took away the central pivot of his social life.

Also, further experiments with grapefruit juice, cherryade, Tizer and other highly priced and highly sweetened fluids had reinforced his opinion that all other forms of beverage, except for tea and coffee, tasted absolutely vile.

It really was becoming very important that he found out quickly who had murdered Warnock Belvedere.

Russ Lavery had the advantage of one of the biggest of the Pinero's dressing rooms, which was set on the corner of the building and therefore had a splendid view out towards Salisbury Plain.

He also had the disadvantage that the dressing room was rather full. As well as Fleance/Young Siward, it housed Malcolm, Donalbain/Seyton, Mentieth and Caithness/ Second Murderer. Since all of these were doubling various messengers, attendants, apparitions and soldiers, the dressing room was going to be even fuller after the costumes had been issued.

When Charles slipped in at the end of the Thursday rehearsal, Russ was sitting somewhat gloomily over in a corner of the dressing room by the window. Mentieth and Caithness/Second Murderer were packing their day's belongings into shoulder bags and talking in that loud, flamboyant manner of young actors which could be gay or could be just theatrical.

They seemed to be ignoring Russ and, as they left the room, nodding at Charles, they pointedly did not say goodbye to the younger actor.

"Wonder if we could have a word . . . ?" said Charles. He hadn't yet worked out how he was going to play the scene, so his opening gambit wasn't particularly original.

But at least Russ responded. "Sure." He moved a chair to make space for his visitor.

"You don't look your most cheery," said Charles, stating no more than the truth. Close to, Russ looked like a vulnerable fourteen-year-old, his eyes moist as if on the verge of tears.

"No," he concurred.

"What is it? Anything you can talk about?"

"Not really."

"You didn't seem to be getting a lot of support from Mentieth and Caithness."

"No."

Charles felt a sudden insight. "They being tough on you because you're new in the business?"

"You could say that." The expression in the boy's eyes told Charles that his guess had been correct.

"I'm afraid that happens. A couple of years out of drama school and they think they know everything."

"And that nobody else knows anything," Russ said bitterly.

"They're getting at you?"

The boy nodded.

"What, saying that the stuff you've done in drama school doesn't count for anything? That you don't know a thing about professional theatre?"

118

"All that. And then when I tell them things, they think I'm showing off."

"What sort of things?"

"Well, like about my agent. . . ."

"Ah."

"I mean, you know, I just mentioned that Robbie Patrick saw me in an end of term show and signed me up, and they think I'm bragging about it."

"He's a very good agent."

"I know."

"I mean, it really is good that he signed you up."

"Yes, I know it is. But they seem to think I go on about it too much. I don't mean to."

"They're just jealous. Who are their agents?"

Russ mentioned a couple of names.

"Oh well, they certainly are jealous," said Charles encouragingly. "Those two are way down the league."

"Yes, so I've heard." Russ managed a weak smile. "Almost as bad as being with Maurice Skellern."

"Oh?" said Charles casually. "Do you know any of Maurice Skellern's clients?"

"No. I've only heard the name."

"In what context?"

"Oh, just as a joke, you know. He's proverbial as the worst agent in the business."

"Ah." Charles decided they might perhaps not pursue this topic further. "So, basically, the others in the dressing room are making you aware of your junior status?"

Russ nodded his head, plunged back into gloom.

"Just saying unpleasant things, or are they doing things too?"

"What do you mean?"

"Practical jokes, anything of that sort . . . ?"

By way of answer, Russ Lavery reached into his jacket pocket and held a folded letter towards Charles.

The notepaper was headed "Robbie Patrick Associates" and Charles read:

"Dear Russ,

Hope you're knocking them dead in Warminster.

Wanted to pass on the great news that the producers want you to test for a part in the new Bond movie. Ring me for details of time, etc.

Yours ever,

Robbie."

He looked up. Now the boy's tears were really flowing. Charles had forgotten just how cruel young actors could be to each other.

"Little sods," he said. "Where did they get the paper from?"

"Easy enough these days with photocopiers," Russ sobbed. "I think they nicked one of Robbie's real letters from my pocket and copied the letterhead."

Yes, there was a faint line across the paper above the type-written text.

"And you fell for it?"

Russ nodded glumly. "Right in. Talked about it, too."

"Oh dear. And rang Robbie?"

"Yes. He thought I was mad. So now I expect I've screwed things up with him as well."

"No, of course you haven't. You've just been the victim of a practical joke. You're sure it was them who did it?"

Russ nodded. "Can't prove anything. But they've been sniggering all day, the bastards."

"Well, look, it's done now. You've given them the satisfaction of falling for it, now you've got to make sure you don't give them any more satisfaction."

"What do you mean?"

"Just never mention it again."

"I suppose you're right. But I'd really like to get my own back on them."

"No. That won't help. Honestly. You'll soon forget all about it."

But Charles's soothing words disguised his very real anger. It had been a vicious trick, and its crudeness simply reinforced the viciousness. Only someone as naive in the business as Russ would have fallen for it. To think that an unknown out of drama school should be screen-tested for a Bond movie . . .

And yet Charles could empathize. He knew that silly bubble of hope trapped inside all actors, which can burst to the surface through any amount of logic and commonsense. He knew that, if he had received that letter, his first reaction would have been to believe it. Then experience and a native cynicism would have dampened his enthusiasm and he would have recognized the cheat.

But poor Russ Lavery hadn't got that protective armour. All he had was the boundless enthusiasm and vulnerability of youth.

"And is that all that's wrong . . . ?" Charles asked tentatively, remembering the purpose of his visit.

The boy shook his head. "Oh, I don't know. There's money . . ."

"There's always money . . ." But it must be hard for a boy trying for the first time to budget on the pittance of Equity minimum. Particularly hard if he's trying to squire around an actress ten years his senior. A couple of flamboyant gestures of buying meals for Felicia could have written off most of his week's pay-packet.

"Well, Russ, I haven't got much, but if you need a fiver to help you out till Friday . . ."

"No, it's all right. I'm okay. I don't want to get into debt."

"Very wise." Charles himself always tried to avoid the endless circle of borrowing from other actors. It so quickly got out of hand, and the reputation of being a sponger was easily acquired.

"No other problems, though?"

Russ looked up defiantly. "Why, what should there be?"

Charles shrugged. Two-and-a-half days into his abstinence, he could now once again shrug with impunity. Maybe that was another of the advantages of not drinking . . . ? On reflection, though, it did seem a pretty small advantage.

"Well, there's always sex . . ." he ventured in answer to Russ's question.

"What do you mean?"

"All the old clichés of sexual angst. Somebody you like rejecting your advances . . . ? Someone you don't like making advances . . . ?"

The boy turned abruptly to look out of the window. "I don't know what you're talking about."

"Listen, I saw the way Warnock was behaving to you that first night."

Russ's eyes flashed back at Charles. "I'm not gay!"

"I never said you were. In fact, just the reverse. I'm saying how embarrassing it must have been for you to have that old queen pawing at you."

The boy shuddered. "Yes, he was horrible. I think the most evil person I've ever come across."

It was quite possible that, in Russ's limited experience, that was true.

"The only good thing that's happened in the last few days," the boy continued, his eyes burning, "is that old bastard's death. He certainly deserved it." This last sentence was spoken in an intriguing tone of satisfaction.

But Charles decided not to probe in that direction for the moment. Instead, infinitely gently, he said, "And then, of course, there's Felicia . . ."

Russ seemed about to flash further defiance at this intrusion, but then subsided into misery. "Yes, there's Felicia. I love her," he confessed abjectly.

"She's a very beautiful girl."

"Yes, but I . . . I think I misunderstood her."

"What do you mean?"

"Well, have you ever . . . I mean, with a woman, have you ever sort of thought you were getting signals from her, and thought you understood those signals, and thought she wanted you to do something . . . and then you've done it—and suddenly realized that wasn't what she meant at all?"

"Yes, I've known that happen. Is that . . . with Felicia . . . ?"

The boy's tears were once again flowing. "I did what I thought she wanted . . . and now she's turned against me . . ."

"Are you talking about Monday night?"

"Yes. Oh, it's just awful. I ruined everything."

"What, you mean you went back to her digs and—"

"No," Russ interrupted fiercely. "No, I didn't."

"Where did you go?"

"I didn't go anywhere. I stayed round the theatre. I don't know what I did."

"Russ, you must tell me if—"

Abruptly Russ Lavery rose to his feet. "I've said too much."

"It's good to talk."

"No. You can't trust people. They suddenly turn on you and then you . . . have to get your own back."

Charles rose from his seat to bar the boy's access to the door. "I'm not going to turn on you, Russ. You can trust me."

"That's what Warnock said," the boy snapped bitterly.

Then in an instant he turned and, reaching for the catch of the window, opened it and slipped out on to the path that skirted the theatre. He was running and out of sight almost before Charles had time to register the movement.

Charles went forward and looked at the window. At the bottom of the frame was an anti-theft device that should have locked down into the sill. But the screw had broken.

In other words, anyone who knew about that window could escape from the theatre when everything was supposedly locked.

Just as it had been on the night of Warnock Belvedere's murder.

So the problem of the murderer's getting out of the locked building had suddenly evaporated.

And, as he had just demonstrated, Russ Lavery clearly knew about the broken window-lock.

Chapter Thirteen

HE KNEW IT was silly to be influenced by *Macbeth*, and yet there was a kind of logic about it. A crime committed by a man, but instigated by a woman. The idea of Felicia Chatterton as an unwitting Lady Macbeth to Russ Lavery's callow Macbeth made an ugly kind of sense.

From the very start of rehearsal, she had found Warnock Belvedere difficult. He had been extremely rude to her in front of the entire company on more than one occasion. Even worse than that from Felicia's point of view, he had threatened the single-minded concentration which was so essential in her build-up to a part.

And she was so obsessive about her work that she would want all obstacles to its progress removed.

No doubt she had said as much to Russ. The poor boy, absolutely besotted with her, excited at the thought not only of embarking on his professional career but also of having an affair with a *real actress*, would have done anything to gain her favour. And, though she probably did no more than express a wish that Warnock might be got out of the way, Russ might have taken her too literally and seen the murder as the ultimate proof of his devotion.

That would tie in with what the boy had said about getting signals from Felicia and misinterpreting them.

"I did what I thought she wanted . . . and now she's turned against me . . ." Yes, it fitted horribly well. After he had committed the murder, Russ had gone to her, figuratively presenting his beautiful Salome with the head of Warnock Belvedere, anticipating presumably some sexual reward for realizing her desires. And she, when she understood what he had done, had recoiled in horror. That would explain the marked estrangement between them after the Monday night.

There were other uncomfortably appealing elements in the theory. Russ did not just have Felicia's promptings as motivation to kill Warnock. The old actor's advances had clearly upset the boy. The vehemence with which Russ had asserted his heterosexuality to Charles betrayed an insecurity about his sexual identity. He was emotionally immature, as his puppylike courtship of Felicia revealed, and he must have been deeply unsettled by Warnock Belvedere's overt importuning. He needed to remove that disturbing challenge from his life.

Charles suddenly recalled Russ's appearance in the storeroom during the Saturday morning runthrough. So there was no doubt that the boy knew what the room was. And, with sickening logic, Charles also remembered Russ saying he had supplemented his grant by working as a barman. He would therefore know all about changing beer barrels and be aware of the potentially lethal presence of carbon dioxide in the gas cylinders.

It was beginning to look painfully likely that Russ Lavery had murdered Warnock Belvedere. The way to check of course was to talk to the poor boy's Lady Macbeth.

"God, I'm just having such difficulty sleeping," Felicia announced, producing yet another parallel for anyone wishing to compare her situation with that of the character she was playing. Charles found himself half-expecting her to continue, "Yet who would have thought the old man to have had so much beer on him", or to sniff distractedly at her fingers and murmur, "Here's the smell of beer still. All the perfumes of Arabia will not sweeten this little hand. Oh! Oh! Oh!"

"Yes, everyone's getting a bit tense. The thought that we open Tuesday week and there's so much to do."

"You can say that again. It's just never going to happen. I mean, I knew it was insane to try and do such a complex piece in three-and-a-half weeks. We need three-and-a-half weeks just talking about it before we even start rehearsal."

"It'll happen," Charles reassured. "It always does happen. Somehow."

"Not always," Felicia disagreed gloomily. "Some productions don't open on time. Particularly of the Scottish Play."

"Oh, come on, you don't believe all that rubbish, do you?"

Her reply came back in a tone of pious reproof. He had challenged one of the articles of her faith in the theatre. "There must be something in it. That sort of rumour doesn't build up for no reason. You hear such terrible stories . . ."

"Like what?"

"Well, this is absolutely authentic, because I know the people involved. Girlfriend of mine was playing Second Witch in Glasgow, and she had a thing with the Banquo. She got pregnant and . . ." the voice dropped to an awestruck murmur ". . . she lost the baby."

"That could be regarded as a coincidence."

"Maybe, but I think there's something else behind it. The Witches' incantations are supposed to be real black magic, you know."

"Yes, I've heard that." Charles spoke dismissively.

"And then I heard of a production when, in the fight at the end, Macduff's sword got knocked out of his hand and flew into the auditorium . . . and impaled someone to their seat in the front row."

"Yes, I've heard that story. Everyone's heard that story. But I've yet to come across anyone who can name the production in which it occurred. It's always something heard from a friend of a friend. I'm sure it never really happened."

"Well, what about this production then?"

"You think this one's got a jinx on it?"

"Oh, come on, Charles. Look at the things that have gone wrong. First, a three-and-a-half week rehearsal period . . ."

"Ah, now I know you think that's hopelessly inadequate, but it's a bit extreme to see that as a manifestation of malign influences. You can blame Gavin's judgement, you can blame the hard economic facts of running a theatre, but to blame the Powers of Evil is really excessive."

"It's not just that, though. Other things . . ."

"Like . . . ?"

"That Macduff's Son not being allowed to continue with the part . . . George being delayed in Paris . . ."

"Those are inconveniences, yes, but they're the kind of things that happen in lots of productions. I don't think they're evidence of a curse on the play."

"And then . . ." The wonderful voice swooped even lower ". . . there's Warnock Belvedere's death."

"Yes," Charles agreed, glad the conversation had moved to that subject of its own accord. "There is something strange about that, certainly . . ."

They were sitting in the bar at the end of the Friday's rehearsal. They had worked hard and knew that they would have to work harder the next day. Gavin was insisting on another Saturday runthrough to fix the shape of the whole play and consolidate what they had done during the week. Straight through the play in the morning, then notes and detailed repair work on bits that weren't right in the afternoon.

Russ Lavery was not in the bar. He had been at rehearsal and done his work, but made no social contact with anyone. Whenever Charles had come near, the boy had taken evasive action.

Charles and Felicia were both sipping chaste Perrier water. Felicia, in her nunlike devotion to her art, very rarely drank alcohol during a rehearsal period. And Charles, of course . . . well, he'd made his pledge, hadn't he?

On his fourth alcohol-free day, after excursions to various other sickly fluids, he had come back to Perrier. With a decent-sized chunk of lemon, it almost began to have a taste.

It wasn't the same, though. Nothing was the same. He looked wistfully across to the bar, where other actors swilled their carefree pints or sipped convivial scotches.

His resolution wavered. The disgusting image of Warnock Belvedere's beer-soaked body was fading. So was the memory of the Tuesday's hangover. One drink wouldn't hurt, surely . . . ?

But no. He had made a vow. Not until he had solved the case. When he knew who the murderer was, then he'd have a drink.

"What were you thinking of doing about eating?"

Felicia's voice brought him out of his alcohol nostalgia. "I'm sorry?"

"Eating. I wondered if you had any plans."

"Not particularly, no."

"Would you like to come back to the cottage? I could rustle up something . . ."

"Oh, that's very kind."

"I always find cooking takes my mind off work. If you don't mind something pretty basic . . ."

"I'd be delighted."

"And I'd like to *talk*," Felicia said earnestly.

Yes, thought Charles. I'd like you to *talk*, too.

It had to be a cottage. It was the RSC background. The villages around Stratford-upon-Avon are full of rented cottages in which actors and actresses stay up late into the night performing microsurgery on Shakespeare's plays and discussing their art, to them so infinitely various and to outsiders so infinitely the same.

So, when Felicia looked for digs for the Pinero job, she homed in on what she knew, and rented a cottage. Her London base was a tiny studio flat in Maida Vale, but she hadn't even gone back there on the free Sundays in the *Macbeth* rehearsal period. She did not want her attention distracted from her ascent of the North Face of Lady Macbeth.

It was a pretty, chintzy little cottage and on arrival she allowed herself the indulgence of a glass of white wine and Perrier. Charles, though sorely tempted, had one without the white wine. In a way, that was the most difficult moment he had encountered in his campaign of temperance. It just seemed so against nature not to have a drink while sitting down waiting to eat.

What Felicia rustled up was lasagne and salad. Very nice, too. Not shop-prepared. The pasta came from a packet, but she cooked it all herself.

Charles could see her through the open kitchen door as she prepared the meal, but she was too far away for continuous conversation. He looked around the room. Let furnished, of course, so she had had little opportunity to impose her personality on the environment.

But there were a few characteristic touches. On a low table in front of the sofa books were piled randomly, some opened, some not. There were at least three different editions of *Macbeth*. The Cambridge *A New Companion to Shakespeare Studies*, *Shakespeare's Macbeth*, *A Selection of Critical Essays*, Edited by John Wain, Terence Hawkes' *Twentieth Century Interpretations of Macbeth*. Felicia Chatterton certainly believed in doing her homework.

On a dresser there was a book on aerobics and another on how to deal with back pain. A couple of cards on the mantelpiece. Charles managed to read their messages without snooping too overtly. Both wishing her good luck for rehearsals. Both evidently from actors and, judging from the in-jokey tone, actors who had been her colleagues at Stratford.

In the otherwise empty fireplace stood a tall vase containing a dozen red roses. A gesture of affection from someone. But there was no sign of a card. A few red petals lay wrinkling on the hearth, so the gesture had probably been made the previous week. By whom? Russ? That would have made heavy inroads into his Equity minimum. But it would have been typical of his romantic naiveté.

As Felicia had said it would, the cooking seemed to relax her, and when she came in holding the two loaded plates and balancing a wooden salad bowl between them, she looked more human and accessible than Charles had ever seen her.

And astonishingly pretty. There must have been a bathroom off the kitchen, because she had clearly titivated herself a bit. For the first time in their acquaintance, she had released her blond hair from its severe knot and it swung, silky and just-brushed, a couple of inches above her shoulders. She had also touched up her lips with the palest of lipsticks, and a breath of expensively fresh perfume preceded her.

Charles wondered whether she made these changes every evening when she returned from rehearsal, or if they were for his benefit.

She gestured to him to rescue the salad bowl, which he placed on the floor. She put the plates beside it and reached for the wine bottle. "Sure you won't, Charles . . . ?"

Ooh, it hurt. But he managed to refuse. Gosh, wouldn't Frances be proud of him. He must ring and tell her of this new miracle. When? Maybe when he'd done it for a week . . . Yes, a week had a good, solid feel to it.

The thought of Frances made him think of sex. Funny, he hardly had thought about it at all in the last week. The shock of Warnock's death, and the hard work of rehearsal seemed to have driven it, atypically, from his mind. At least, he hoped that was the reason. It could, of course, just be that he was getting old. Like many men before him, he suffered a momentary panic at the idea that something he'd so frequently cursed as a troublesome distraction might be about to cease troubling him.

Or maybe it was because he was off the booze . . . Now that really was a terrifying thought. He tried to recall whether previous bouts of abstinence had had this bromide effect on his libido. Trouble was, he couldn't recall any previous bouts of abstinence.

Felicia sat beside him on the sofa. She didn't suggest moving her *Macbeth* library from the low table and they ate off their knees.

The lasagne was good, creamy and spicy. They were both hungry after the day's hard work and ate in silence. Charles chased the last strip of lettuce round his plate and leaned back in satisfaction.

"That was really good. Thanks."

"Would you like some fruit? I've got apples and kiwi-fruit. Or there's yoghourt . . . ?"

"No, thanks. That was fine. Just right."

"Coffee? You do drink coffee, don't you?"

"Yes. In a minute, if you're having some. But there's no hurry."

She finished her last mouthful and put the plate down on the floor. She too leant back, grimacing as she stretched against the sofa.

"Back bad?"

She nodded. "Hmm. I know it's just tension. Always happens through rehearsals. Every vertebra seems to lock into the next one. I do exercises, but it still seizes up."

"Has it ever stopped you going on?"

She looked at him in amazement. "Good heavens, no. As soon as I get on stage I don't feel a thing. I can do really elaborate movement stuff without a twinge."

"Doctor Theatre strikes again."

"That's right. Oh, I know it's psychosomatic, really. Doesn't make it any the less painful."

"No."

"What kind of symptoms do you get?"

"Sorry?"

"Anxiety symptoms. You know, running up to a first night."

"Oh." Charles would have liked to say he got none. His pose of world-weary cynicism should put him above such self-indulgent frailties. But he knew that it didn't. "Tends to go to my stomach. Always think I'm about to throw up just before a first night."

"Do you ever?"

"Have done. Not for a while."

"Do you know any actors who don't get nervous?"

Charles shook his head. "Nope. I always feel with the ones who keep insisting that they don't, it's just their own way of expressing the nervousness. They go on about it so much."

"Yes."

There was a companionable lull in the conversation. Their mutual confession of nerves seemed to have made a bridge between them. Charles wondered how he was going to steer the conversation round to Russ Lavery and Warnock Belvedere's death. But he didn't wonder with any great urgency.

He glanced across at Felicia's head, near his on the sofa. Her eyes were closed as she relaxed and the little furrows, which during rehearsal became a fixture on her brow, had been smoothed away. She looked very young. Such soft, smooth skin.

He realized, with ironical relief, that the anxiety he had had before the meal was groundless. He was quite capable of thinking about sex without alcoholic prompting.

In fact, he was thinking about it quite a lot.

To divert his thoughts from that particular track, he deliberately moved the conversation back to his murder investigation. He must behave himself. Perhaps his new image of abstinence should carry over into his sex-life, too. Mr Clean. No vices. Proper little Sir Galahad, he thought. "My strength is as the strength of ten, because my heart is pure." Hmm. It had some appeal. Not much, though. Sir Galahad's life may have been jolly pure, but it never sounded as if it had been much *fun*. All very well, in principle, devoting all your time to one long-term Grail; Charles preferred the idea of picking up a few nice little lesser Grails on the way.

As if it couldn't have mattered less, he floated a new topic of conversation. "Felicia, about Warnock Belvedere's death . . ."

Chapter Fourteen

THE CHANGE OF subject did not seem to upset her. She still lay back on the sofa with her eyes closed, and said nothing.

"I think very few people were sorry to hear about it," Charles continued.

"I certainly wasn't," Felicia agreed sleepily. "He was making my life impossible."

"Oh?"

"Not just the rudeness. I could ignore that. But his constant interruptions made concentration so difficult. And I am trying to get inside Lady Macbeth," she said, confirming what Charles had thought earlier. "In fact, it was just as well that he did die when he did."

Charles rationed himself to just another "Oh?"

"Well, I'd given Gavin an ultimatum. I said either Warnock would have to go or I would."

"Yes, I heard you say that to him after last Saturday's run. I didn't know you'd meant it literally."

"Oh, I meant it. I said it again on the Monday. Saw Gavin on his own and told him that if Warnock was at rehearsal the next morning, I was going to have to leave the company."

"Really?"

"I know that sounds unprofessional, threatening to break a contract, but you can only be professional if other people around you are being professional. Warnock Belvedere was sabotaging any chance I had of building a performance."

"Yes." Charles allowed a cosy pause to develop before he continued diffidently. "So Warnock's death was quite timely for you."

"Couldn't have been more timely. I really meant what I said.

If he had still been there on the Tuesday, I would have walked out. He was an obstructive, offensive old man, and death was the best thing that could have happened to him."

This was spoken so openly that it seemed to Charles to absolve Felicia from suspicion of direct involvement in the murder. But the possibility still remained that she had, either knowingly or unknowingly, inspired someone else to commit the crime.

"Did anyone else know how strongly you felt about Warnock?"

"I didn't make a secret of it. Anyone could have worked it out for themselves."

"Hmm. What about Russ?"

The mention of this name broke her serenity. The eyelids snapped open to reveal, unnervingly close to Charles, the concentrated blue of her eyes. The little furrows were once again etched between her eyebrows. "What do you mean?"

Charles shrugged. "I just meant, did Russ know how much you wanted Warnock out of the way?"

"Yes. Of course he did. We . . . we talked a lot about the production. I told Russ that I couldn't go on unless somehow Warnock was got out of the way."

"You said that? You used those exact words?"

"Something like that, certainly."

Again the ingenuousness of her reply seemed to rule her out as a suspect, and even as a deliberate prompter to murder. She had told Russ in all innocence that she wanted her tormentor "got out of the way". But how the blindly besotted youth might have interpreted her remark was another matter.

She arched her body and brought back her elbows behind her to alleviate the pain in her spine. "Ooh, gosh, it's tense," she said, as she did so.

"Bad luck," Charles commiserated, trying to think of something other than the splendid way in which that posture accentuated her breasts.

Once again, he moved his thoughts away from sex by pressing

on with the investigation. "Russ is rather keen on you, isn't he?"

She diminished the idea with a gesture. "Oh. Maybe a bit. I don't know. We certainly got on well, talking, you know. He's a very intelligent boy. He sees Lady Macbeth in very much the same way as I do."

"Ah. You don't think it's possible, do you, Felicia, that he—?"

Abruptly she stood up. "Ooh, Charles, sorry. This back's just so tight. And my shoulders. I say, would you mind just massaging it a bit?"

"No, I wouldn't mind," he replied, very honestly.

"Thanks."

She moved the table of *Macbeth* books and lay flat on the carpet in front of the sofa. "If you don't mind just kneeling or . . ."

"No problem. Where, right down the spine itself? Like that?"

"Yes, and sort of easing off to either side. Yes, you can really press down on it. It needs a lot of pressure. Ooh, that's nice."

Charles thought it was rather nice, too. Her spine was quite prominent through the soft cotton of her track suit, but there was no transverse ridge of a brassiere. And the flesh was comfortingly soft.

He permanently revised his opinion about his interest in sex being dependent on the intake of alcohol.

But he wondered why she was behaving like this. It could be completely innocent, just the behaviour of someone with a bad back, or it could be one of the most blatant come-ons he had ever encountered. He was not yet quite sure which.

Of course, it had had the effect of breaking off the conversation about Russ, and Charles began to wonder whether maybe that had been its primary intention.

But he was determined not to be sidetracked. "Felicia, about you and Russ . . ."

"I really don't want to talk about it." Her voice was muffled by her arms on which she was lying, but he could feel its resonance with his kneading fingertips.

"I do want to talk about it."

"Why?"

He decided there was no point in going the pretty way. "Because I think it might have something to do with Warnock's death."

She raised her head and squinted round at him. "What on earth do you mean?"

"Felicia, most of last week you and Russ were as thick as thieves . . ."

"So . . . ?"

"But nobody in the company could fail to notice that on Tuesday morning you didn't want to have anything to do with him."

She coloured and turned her head back towards the floor. "Surely that's my business."

"Well, yes, it's your business, so long as it doesn't start involving other people."

"It doesn't involve other people. Just Russ and me."

"Listen. I've been asking myself—what happened between closing time in the bar on Monday and the start of rehearsals on Tuesday . . ."

"It's none of your business what—"

". . . and the only thing that I *know* happened between those times," Charles went on inexorably, "was that Warnock Belvedere died."

"But that's nothing to do with Russ and me."

"By your own admission, you wanted Warnock out of the way . . ."

"Yes."

"And wasn't the timing of his 'getting out of the way' rather convenient?"

"Yes, it was, but . . ." She rolled over and sat up, facing him. The eyes were disconcertingly beautiful. "What are you on about, Charles?"

136

He had to play this carefully. He wanted to find out certain facts, but he didn't want Felicia to be frightened off by the direction of his questions. He opted for a straightforward lie. "Listen, I was the one who found Warnock's body . . ."

"I know that."

". . . and, because I was presumably in the theatre when he died, the police have been asking me various questions." All true so far. Time for the lie. "In particular, they've asked me if I saw anyone else round the theatre at the relevant time." He hoped she didn't remember that he had been out cold at the time he was supposed to be observing.

She appeared not to. "I don't see how I can help you."

"You can help me by telling me what you did after the bar closed that evening."

"I came straight back here."

"Yes, I thought you probably did. What is more pertinent, really, is: Do you know what Russ did?"

She hesitated. "Why don't you ask him?"

"I have done."

"Well, then you know the answer." She had a moment of doubt. "What did he tell you he did?"

"He said he stayed around the theatre for a while."

The answer seemed somehow to please her. "Then you know what he did, don't you?" She shuffled round so that she was sitting with her back to him. "Charles, would you mind just doing a bit on the shoulders? The spine feels much better, but the shoulders are still really knotted."

"Sure." His fingers started to slide back and forth across the material of her track suit. As the sweeps grew broader, the fingers touched the soft perfumed flesh of her neck with each stroke. The sweeps grew broader still.

"Ooh, that's lovely," she purred. She eased her neck luxuriantly round, and a few wisps of hair tickled across his chin.

"Thing is, though," Charles continued gently, "the police are going to question me closely about who I saw. Russ apparently was there, but I didn't see him."

137

"Probably in his dressing room," Felicia mumbled.

"The other thing is . . . if the police did know Russ was around the theatre, they might want to question him."

"Why?"

No way round it. He'd have to be more direct. "Has it ever occurred to you that Warnock's death might not have been an accident?"

"What—you mean that he might have been murdered?" The tone of incredulity sounded genuine. Either the idea never had occurred to her, or she was a very good actress. But then, of course, Charles reflected, she *was* a very good actress.

"It's a possibility that I'm sure the police must have considered."

She turned her head round to look at him. "And you mean, if they knew that Russ had been in the theatre at the time, they might suspect him of the murder?"

"Possible. Isn't it?"

The look of shock on her face seemed genuine, too. Maybe Russ had told her he had killed Warnock and she hadn't believed it, thought the boy was showing off, fantasizing. But now she was having his story confirmed from another source, and that was frightening her.

There was a long silence. Then, in the deep voice which had so captivated Stratford theatregoers, she announced, "Russ didn't stay around the theatre."

"Oh."

She knew she had to tell him more. "He came back here, with me."

"Straight after closing time?"

"Yes, I drove him here."

"Oh well, that's fine. Lets him off the hook then, doesn't it?" Charles was surprised at the depth of his relief. He hadn't enjoyed casting Russ Lavery in the role of murderer. The boy was too young, too appealing, had too much ahead of him to do such a thing. Besides, Charles liked him, and he didn't enjoy unmasking murderers he liked.

So it had just been a secret lovers' assignation. Russ's devotion had paid off. He had achieved the prize which John B. Murgatroyd had jokingly set his sights on.

But, as well as relief, Charles couldn't help feeling a twinge of jealousy. Felicia was very lovely.

She turned her back towards him again. "Do you mind going on? It really is working."

"Knitting up the ravell'd sleave of care, am I?" he asked with a grin, as he fingered the sleeve of her tracksuit.

"That's it." She let out a little contented sigh. She was comfortable with Shakespearean quotations. And they weren't in a theatre, so *Macbeth* could be quoted with impunity.

Charles's fingers worked round the neck and shoulders, sweeping in ever wider and wider arcs. She nuzzled back against him, though whether this was merely to make herself comfortable or with a view to making him comfortable too, he could still not decide.

"One thing's odd . . ." he murmured.

"What's that?"

"Why didn't Russ tell me he came back here with you?"

"Oh, I don't know . . ."

Obviously she did know, but it didn't seem too important to Charles, as the curves described by his fingertips moved lower and lower. Ho, ho, ho, John B. Murgatroyd, I may have something to tell you tomorrow that'll make you green with envy.

"Actually," Felicia announced in a voice that was informative rather than admonitory, "it's just the neck and shoulders that are tense. My breasts are fine."

"You took the words right out of my mouth," mumbled Charles as he moved his face forward to nestle in her soft hair.

She gently disengaged herself, and looked at him.

"Shall I tell you why Russ lied about what happened?"

"Sure. I'd be interested."

"We were talking about *Macbeth* in the bar and I was telling him about one of the essays in this book." She indicated *A New*

Companion to Shakespeare Studies. "He sounded interested, so I invited him to come back for a coffee and have a look at it."

"Ah."

"Unfortunately, he didn't understand what I meant."

"Oh." Another embarrassment arising from the fatal ambiguity of the word "coffee". Charles found he was now avoiding Felicia's eyes.

"Russ thought I was inviting him to come to bed with me."

"Oh dear."

"It was embarrassing. He's very young. He took it as a personal slight."

"I'm afraid men often do," Charles mumbled.

"I couldn't make him understand that it wasn't just him. It was any man."

For a moment Charles wondered if he was about to receive a confession of lesbianism, but Felicia's next words fortunately cleared that up.

"Not while I'm in rehearsal," she said, speaking of the mystery in an awed voice.

"You mean . . ." asked Charles, having difficulty piecing the idea together ". . . you don't have sex while you're rehearsing?"

"No. I find it spoils my concentration."

"Oh."

"Don't you?"

"What—find it spoils my concentration?"

"Yes."

"Well, no, I don't think I do, really. Seems to help it, actually . . ."

But she didn't pick up the hint and volunteer to experiment with this novel approach. "No, I just can't do it," she said.

Charles, whose recent edifice of plans for the rest of the evening had just crumbled in jerry-built chaos, was intrigued. "What about when you're actually running . . . you know, when a show's on . . . do you find you can manage it then?"

She shook her head. "Very rarely. I have tried, but it still does affect the concentration."

Hmm. Charles hoped she wasn't very highly sexed. If she was, and insisted on maintaining this Spartan discipline, she had certainly chosen the wrong profession. And all that time at Stratford . . . Working in repertory, getting one show on and going straight into rehearsal for another . . . good heavens, it must have been years since she had had anything.

Poor Russ. Barking up the wrong tree.

Never mind. At least the boy wasn't a murderer.

"Actually, Charles, there was a reason why I invited you back here this evening . . ."

Oh well, that was nice to know. He wondered what it was. Not just the massage, surely. And definitely not sex. What? Maybe the odd light-bulb needed changing.

"No, it's because you're an educated man . . ."

That was different, at least.

"You read English at Oxford, didn't you?"

"Yes. Over thirty years ago, though."

"Well, I wanted to ask you about the interpretation of some of Lady Macbeth's lines." She eagerly pulled the table of books across towards them. "I mean, particularly the 'I have given suck' problem."

"The 'I have given suck' problem?"

"Yes, I mean it's a crux which has been discussed for centuries. Because of course it's at odds with Macduff's 'He has no children'."

"Of course." It dawned on Charles that, now Russ had blotted his copybook, Felicia was in need of someone else to discuss her work with. He groaned inwardly as he realized that he had drawn this particular short straw.

"So, you see, I think you have to get into Lady Macbeth this sense of bereavement, because clearly she has had a child which has died in infancy."

"Ah."

"But this raises particular problems in some of her scenes with Macbeth. And when we first see her and she speaks of 'the milk of human-kindness', surely she must feel a pang, thinking of her own milk which was inadequate to sustain the life of her child. Incidentally, of course, there's quite a valid alternative reading of that as 'the milk of *humane* kindness', which, I'm sure you agree, puts a rather different complexion on . . ."

Felicia Chatterton continued for some time. Charles provided the occasional agreement or grunt, but she didn't seem to need them.

After a time, his chin sank on to his chest. His eyes closed and he slipped easily into a comfortable slumber.

Oblivious, Felicia Chatterton talked on.

Chapter Fifteen

CHARLES SPENT A restless weekend after the Saturday run-through. John B. Murgatroyd had offered another Sunday tour of the locals of the locality, but the idea of comparing the size of the lemon slices with which various pubs garnished their Perrier water did not appeal. So John B. went off with a couple of other actors from the company, leaving Charles feeling like the last child in the playground to be picked for either team.

He felt restless about Frances, too. He must make contact with her. But he'd promised himself a week of abstinence before he did, and he'd had his last drink at closing time on the previous Monday.

Even as he worked these sums out, though, he knew he was deceiving himself, and he came round reluctantly to the idea that he was actually afraid of contacting Frances. Her unwillingness to see him made him feel raw and adolescent again, fearing another rebuff. It was stupid to feel like that about his wife.

And yet he had to admit that Frances had put up with a lot. But always before, when he had suddenly turned up again in her life, she had been wryly welcoming. Now, for the first time, he wondered whether she actually meant what she said about their being better off permanently apart. Maybe she really could get on with her own life more effectively without the ever-present threat of her husband's reappearance.

It was a bleakly plausible possibility, and thinking about it did little to improve his mood. Her determination not to see him, combined with his own natural dilatoriness, could actually mean that they might never meet again.

Picking at the scab, he indulged this painful fantasy. Yes, it could easily happen. And then, finally, one of them would hear of the other's death through a third party. If Frances died, he would hear from his daughter, Juliet, from whom he now seemed to be equally estranged.

And if he died, how would Frances hear about it? His stature in the theatre would not warrant newspaper obituaries. Maurice Skellern would know, obviously, but Charles couldn't envisage his agent taking the trouble to contact Frances. (Actually, given the nature of their relationship, Charles could imagine some months elapsing before Maurice even realized his client was dead.)

He also wondered what their respective reactions would be to the news. Maybe, by the time it happened, Frances would have achieved the hermetic isolation from him that she seemed to crave, and be able to greet the event with a single philosophical tear.

If it were the other way round, he knew that hearing of Frances's death would tear him apart. She still meant so much to him.

"I must make contact with her," he thought desperately. Even as he thought it, though, he added the automatic rider, "but not quite yet."

It wasn't just thoughts of Frances that dampened his spirits. There was also the unsolved murder at the Pinero to trouble him.

There hadn't been much evidence of the police round the theatre in the latter half of the previous week, but Charles didn't feel confident that they had completed their investigations. He still had the uncomfortable sense of being under suspicion. There was to be an inquest on Warnock Belvedere on the Monday morning, and he was anxious about the findings of that inquest.

Also, he didn't like the direction in which the compass of his own suspicions was pointing. Granted, the crime might have been the work of an outsider. Russ Lavery's revelation of the broken window-lock opened up all kinds of alternative possibilities; anyone in the company could have concealed himself (or herself) in the dressing room area, killed Warnock and escaped at will.

But the most likely suspects remained those who had been present in the bar when Norman called "Time" the previous Monday evening. If one excluded elaborate conspiracy theories, Lady Macduff and the two Witches were out of the reckoning. The two couples, Norman and Sandra Phipps, and Felicia and Russ, both had mutual alibis, the one of sexual indulgence, the other of sexual abstinence.

Which left only Gavin Scholes.

He was uniquely positioned from the point of view of opportunity. He knew the Pinero inside out, he had his own keys. And, Charles kept remembering, he had been wide awake in the middle of the night when phoned with the news of Warnock's death.

With regard to motivation, the old actor had been a serious threat to the director's authority. By the Monday Gavin was beginning to lose control of the production, and Warnock Belvedere's constant sniping was fomenting disaffection within the company. Also, Charles now knew, Felicia Chatterton was actually threatening to walk out of rehearsals if Warnock were not removed. And, though replacing a Macduff's Son, or even a Duncan, was not an insurmountable problem, replacing a Lady Macbeth at that notice would have been nearly impossible.

After the disasters of that Monday's rehearsal, Gavin might well have contemplated desperate measures to regain control of his production.

Charles didn't like thinking ill of his old friend, but it was a matter of survival. If the inquest concluded that Warnock Belvedere had been murdered, the prime suspect for that crime was Charles Paris, and he might only be able to escape that charge by producing an alternative murderer.

He decided to watch Gavin Scholes very closely over the next few days.　　　＊

The results of the inquest were good news and bad news. The good news was that the coroner did not reach a verdict of murder. The bad news was that he did not reach any verdict at all. The inquest was adjourned to give the police time to complete their investigations.

That was not very comforting for Charles, implying as it inevitably did that the police had further investigations to make. He wondered anxiously how long it would be before he was hauled out of rehearsal for another little chat with Detective Inspector Dowling.

But the Pinero Theatre's *Macbeth* was gaining momentum, and he had little time to brood. It was a long time since he had been so involved in a production. Charles was used to long lulls in rehearsal, while he sat vaguely watching the principals being coached, drinking too many cups of coffee, sharing whispered professional gossip with other lesser members of the company, whingeing about agents and the Inland Revenue, or toying with *The Times* crossword.

But there was very little chance for all that in *Macbeth*. Though none of his roles was a principal one, Charles had so many of them that he was rarely off the stage, and when he was, he was preoccupied trying to remember where the hell, and in what identity, he had to come on next.

The silly, optimistic fantasy grew that some sharp-eyed critic might recognize his prodigious work-rate. "Charles Paris presented an amazing gallery of characters, each one so subtly distinguished from the others that I had to check my programme to assure myself they really all were the work of one actor." Yes, that'd do. Or how about . . . "Charles Paris demonstrated a Protean ability which stands comparison with that of Olivier"? Or maybe—

He curbed his galloping thoughts. No, be realistic, Charles. Remember the last time you played more than two parts in a production. What was it the *Lancashire Evening Post* had said?

"It's no secret that the theatre's hard up, but to have Charles

Paris shambling on giving the same performance as three supposedly different characters seems to be a false economy."

The mood of a company goes through many changes during a rehearsal period. There is the initial diffidence, frequently followed by a flood of confidence if the first few days rehearsal go well. This quickly gives way to total despair at the first set-back, which usually coincides with the cast "getting off the book" and suddenly, in the desperate hunt for lines, forgetting all the subtleties they so easily performed with scripts in their hands.

This is frequently followed by a period of doldrums, when the progress of the production is so slow as to seem imperceptible. That may well give way to another nadir of despair after a runthrough in which everything goes wrong.

Then, with a bit of luck, comes a sunny period of mounting confidence, as performances burgeon and the company begins to feel that really, after all, the show could be pretty bloody good. This mood will be bolstered by a good director, building the self-esteem of his cast, following that golden rule of all creative work that, even if part of you knows it's rubbish, for the period of most intense hard work you have to suppress that feeling and convince yourself that it's worth doing.

This fragile, but sometimes aggressively confident attitude is usually destroyed in the week before the opening by technical problems. The set, when actually erected on stage, bears no relation to the proportions of the furniture which has represented it for some weeks. Bulky costumes do not allow entrances which have been glibly rehearsed from Day One. Real props turn out to be the wrong shape for bits of business which worked perfectly well with rehearsal props. Doors will not open, swords will not come out of scabbards, helmets blindfold their wearers, cauldrons do not fit over the trap-doors for which they are designed. Anything that can go wrong goes wrong.

And that's before you get on to the problems raised by lighting.

Any pace that has been injected into the production goes, and with it the company confidence slinks away. It seems impossible that the show can ever open. No, never in a thousand years. And if it does manage to, then it shouldn't. It should be put out of its misery now, its sickly life terminated by a quick humane decision of the management. It's going to be the naffest, most incompetent, most amateur-looking production that has ever disgraced the boards of a theatre.

This mood shifts to a stoicism through the long torture of the first (and in many cases last) technical run, during which everything gets slower and slower as the company works deeper into the small hours, and the director, who's been up most of the night before plotting the lights, presses doggedly on, shutting his mind to what it's costing in overtime.

Then a dress rehearsal (or if they're lucky, more than one dress rehearsal), unsatisfactory for the actors however it goes. If it's good, they feel falsely reassured . . . first night bound to be a disappointment. If it's bad, they can comfort themselves with the old cliché about bad dress rehearsals. But that comfort is inadequate, too. Suppose the magic doesn't work this time. Suppose this time a bad dress rehearsal prefigures an even worse first night.

Then the seesawing from manic elation to nauseous panic of the opening day, the false bonhomie, the snapping nerves, the anticipated surprise of cards and presents. And the awful elasticity of time, moving too fast for the urgent things that still need doing, not moving at all for those of the company who have nothing to do but wait.

This is the day for private rituals, for walking to the theatre by special routes, for avoiding certain totems and seeking out others, for touching long-treasured mascots. For many, it is also the day of vowing to leave the profession, swearing that it's an inhuman strain, that it's ridiculous to put oneself under such intolerable emotional pressure.

And, finally, all of that is forgotten in the release of actual performance. Good or bad, however many reputations have been made or lost, however much work is still needed, at least the bloody thing has happened.

All of these changes, all of these swings of mood, all of these alternating images of triumph and disaster, were experienced by the Pinero company in the run-up to the opening of their production of *Macbeth*.

For Charles Paris, the most daunting moment of the third week of rehearsal came when his dressing room door was pushed open to admit a huge bundle of clothes, which advanced panting towards him.

"Um, can I help you?" he asked, uncertain of the appropriate way to address a bundle of clothes.

He heard the muffled word, "Wardrobe," which suggested that the bundle of clothes had a voice. When he looked towards the floor, he saw that it also had feet wearing grubby tennis shoes.

"I'll just put them down on the table."

The bundle of clothes heaved up in the air for a moment, then flopped down on to the dressing room table to reveal a gormless-looking girl with orange-streaked hair and a designer-torn black T-shirt.

"Those are all mine, are they?" asked Charles.

"Yes." The girl picked up each of the garments as she itemized them in an impassively nasal voice. "Right, Bleeding Sergeant."

A leather jerkin, irregularly decorated with metal rings, and a pair of rough hopsack trousers. Those're going to tickle, thought Charles gloomily.

"What about the blood? Do you mind if this lot gets covered in Kensington Gore?" he asked.

"Kensington who?"

"Stage blood."

"Oh, nobody said anything about that. I don't think they'll want blood on the costumes."

"He is a *Bleeding* Sergeant. Shakespeare did specify that in the stage directions."

"I don't care what anyone else said. I take my orders from the Wardrobe Mistress."

Charles did not bother to argue. "All right. I'll try to keep the blood just on my face and forearms. A few nice gashes, I think." He relished the challenge of doing the gashes. Like being back in the old days of really elaborate make-up. That was the trouble with all this modern lighting, you hardly needed any slap, no matter what part you were doing. Still, a gash could be fun. Build up something gruesome with nose-putty. Even latex, yes. Then discolour the jagged edges with a touch of Lake, slap on the old Leichner's Arterial Blood and—

Oh no, sod it. That would only work for someone who wasn't about to enter in Act One Scene Seven as a Sewer. Shakespeare just didn't think ahead, did he? If only he'd written, "Enter a Bleeding Sewer", as well. As it was, Charles would have to settle for less elaborate wounds.

The girl with the orange-streaked hair held up a long dark-blue velvet garment that looked like a mangy housecoat. "For the Sewer."

"Looks a bit grubby. The Macbeths aren't on the breadline, you know."

"Be all right under the lights."

"Oh yes?"

But she wasn't going to be diverted. "I've checked with Gavin. Very low lighting for that scene."

Before Charles could pursue his objection, she raised a stained crimson jerkin and a pair of stained crimson slashed breeches from the pile. "That's the Porter."

"But I'll never be able to do up that jacket."

"You're not meant to. If you have it undone and stick your stomach out, you'll look fat and debauched."

Charles flicked at his eyebrow in mock-affectation. "Oh dear, love, another character part."

But the girl from Wardrobe seemed to have been inoculated

150

against jokes. She lifted up a full-length russet-coloured brocade gown. "Old Man who talks to Ross in Act Two Scene Four."

"What do I wear under it?"

"You can put it on over your Porter costume. It won't show."

"But the shoes will."

"Audience won't notice shoes."

"I'm not thinking of the audience." He dropped into his best theatrical knight voice. "I'm thinking of *me*. You know, a lot of actors say, Get the shoes right and then you get the characterization right."

Once again the attempt at humour was ignored. "As the Third Murderer you wear this."

It was a ragged garment of greenish net, like the sort of stuff used to camouflage aircraft in the jungle in B-movies.

"Just that?"

"Yes. Gavin says the lighting's very dim."

Not just the lighting, thought Charles.

The girl held up an object which at a Fancy Dress party might have passed for a coal-scuttle.

"Um. Let me guess . . ." said Charles. "Scottish Doctor carries that, in case Lady Macbeth's sick in the Sleepwalking Scene . . . ?"

"No, it's what you wear as an Apparition of an Armed Head."

"Just that? But I'm going to be seen from the waist up."

"It said 'Armed Head' in the notes Gavin gave me. Nothing about the rest of the body. Anyway, I thought you were in the cauldron."

"The cauldron only comes up to my waist."

"Then you'll have to crouch. This one . . ." she produced a long white nightshirt ". . . is what you wear as the English Doctor. And this . . ." She produced an identical garment in black ". . . is what you wear as the Scottish Doctor."

Finally, she indicated a mass of silver-painted dishcloth chain-mail, a noisome sleeveless sheepskin jerkin and a horned helmet. "And that lot's for when you're a soldier."

"But I have to be two soldiers," Charles objected.

"What?"

"I have to be on Malcolm's side, and then on Macbeth's side."

"Oh." The girl was momentarily stumped, but then saw a solution. "You can turn the jerkin inside out."

"Oh, what?" said Charles. "You mean really be a turncoat?" She didn't get that one either.

Oh, the pain of the first night party!

God alone knew how many first night parties he had attended, but Charles Paris was certain this was the first one he had attended without benefit of alcohol.

He felt sacrilegious, as if he were offending some basic tenet of his professional faith, sitting there in the bar watching the ice melt in his Perrier, while around him wine and beer glasses were tipped and emptied.

John B. Murgatroyd leant close over him, breathing out tantalizing fumes of bitter. "I felt, Charles Paris, that I had to say I thought your Drunken Porter this evening was masterly."

"Thank you."

"You had me remarkably convinced that you were smashed out of your skull."

"Acting, mere acting," Charles confessed modestly.

George Birkitt was sitting near by, knocking back the red wine. "Of course," he said, appropriating a line that had been said of Lee Marvin's drunken performance in *Cat Ballou*, "it's the part you have been rehearsing for the last forty years."

"But such a remarkable performance," John B. continued in a tone of theatrical preciousness, "from a teetotaller."

"Oh, shut up," said Charles.

"What I fail to understand . . ." John B. had now dropped into a surprisingly accurate pastiche of Felicia Chatterton's earnest huskiness, ". . . is how you could give a performance of such *truth* without *being* the role. I mean, in other words, how you could *appear* so pissed without actually *being* pissed."

Charles took the opportunity to redirect the conversation. "A propos of nothing, how is the get-Felicia-into-bed campaign going?"

John B. touched a finger against the side of his nose knowingly. "Slowly, but surely. At my current rate of progress, I am not unhopeful of achieving my end—or should I say 'getting my end away'—within the next three millennia."

Charles chuckled. "Rather what I found."

"Did you, you dirty devil?" John B. slipped back into Felicia's voice for the next line. "Of course, one could only do it if it were *right for the part*."

"Of course. And that being the case, the only one who's in with any chance of scoring is dear old George."

"Oh, really?" said George Birkitt, misunderstanding, and preening back his hair as if about to open another supermarket. "Whole thing seemed to go rather damned well tonight, I thought. Never expected to get a round on my first entrance."

This had been the work of a little claque of television sit com fans, who had greeted their hero's appearance with unruly ecstasy. Once he started speaking Shakespeare, they had grown noticeably quieter.

"No, went well for all of us," said George, remembering the magnanimity which distinguishes great stars. "Damned clever little actress, that Felicia, isn't she?"

Yes, way out of your league, Charles thought. He had been deeply impressed by Felicia that night. Given the stimulus of an audience, her performance had gone up several notches. Her talent was awesome. Felicia Chatterton would go far.

He looked across at her. Talking earnestly to Russ. Oh well, that was nice. No doubt, having been let down so badly by her substitute confidant's having gone to sleep, Felicia was returning to what she knew would be a ready audience. They could soon get over the embarrassment of their previous misunderstanding.

And, who could say, now the play had actually opened, maybe Russ would be in with a chance . . . ? Charles doubted it, though. A role as demanding as Lady Macbeth was going to take all her concentration. He rather suspected that the only way to have an affair with Felicia Chatterton would be to book it with her agent six months in advance.

"Smashing, all of you. All the hard work's paid off. I can't thank you enough." Gavin Scholes had joined them, full of relief and bonhomie.

Also more than a little drunk. A lot of quick alcohol, after two days of eating only the odd sandwich, combined with the relief of actually having opened the play, had left him cheerfully glazed and indiscreet.

"No, you all came up trumps. Terrific. Can't thank you enough. Because God knows I needed this show to be a success."

"Oh?" asked Charles diffidently.

"Having a bit of trouble with the Board. Money, you know. Not getting enough bums on seats. To be quite frank, my job was on the line. If this show hadn't worked, I could have been out on my ear."

If that were the case, thought Charles, Warnock Belvedere's disruptive presence must have been even more of a threat. His file of motivation for Gavin Scholes grew.

The mutual congratulation continued for a while, and then George Birkitt and John B. Murgatroyd drifted away to chat up the prettier two Witches.

When they were alone, Gavin looked at Charles and his eyes seemed slowly to find their focus. "Charles, that policeman was round the office again today."

"Detective Inspector Dowling?"

The director nodded. "Wants to have another talk with you."

"Oh yes?" was all he said, but the news gave Charles an unpleasant *frisson*. "When?"

"He'll be around tomorrow afternoon. Four-thirty or so. Wondered if you'd mind having a chat between the Schools Matinee and the evening show."

"No problem," said Charles with an insouciance that didn't go very deep.

"I wonder what he wants . . . ?"

Charles shrugged.

"Presumably he's still investigating Warnock's death," Gavin mused. "I thought they'd had the inquest."

"They have, but it was adjourned pending police enquiries."

"What does that mean?"

"Well, I assume it means that the police haven't yet worked out what they think about the case."

Gavin's fuddled mind was having difficulty grasping simple ideas. "Why, what could they think?"

"Well, they could think it was an accident . . ."

"Yes."

"Or they could think it was murder."

Gavin's jaw sagged. "You don't believe that they really think that, do you?"

"I don't know what they think. Presumably I will find that out tomorrow."

"But why you? What can you tell them?"

"I was there, wasn't I? I'm their only possible witness."

"Yes, but you were dead drunk all the time, weren't you?"

"Suppose the police thought I wasn't telling the truth . . . ? Suppose they thought I just pretended to be out cold . . . ?"

The conclusion to Charles's unfinished sentences was, in his mind, that he might then become the police's number one murder suspect. But Gavin's shocked face suggested the director hadn't reached the same conclusion, and his words confirmed it. "You mean you could have actually seen anything that did go on?"

"If I'd been awake, yes, I could have done," said Charles, unnerved by the look in Gavin's eyes and trying to lighten the conversation. "But I was dead to the world. Really."

"Dead to the world," the director echoed. His eyes narrowed as he said, "I hope you really were. For your sake."

Chapter Sixteen

HIS IMPERSONATION OF Felicia Chatterton was now becoming one of John B. Murgatroyd's party pieces. "But it's just so *difficult*," he complained huskily in the dressing room on the Wednesday afternoon, "to try and give a full performance at this time of day. I mean, one's *body-clock* is tuned to peak round eight in the evening, not straight after lunch."

Charles chuckled, but he could see that Felicia, whom John B. was quoting verbatim, had a point. Matinees are welcomed by few actors. They make for a very long, hard day's work. And they always leave that awkward gap between afternoon and evening performance, not long enough to do anything properly, not long enough to wind down fully before winding oneself up again.

But of course on that particular day, Charles Paris had an engagement to bridge the gap. Detective Inspector Dowling. It was not an engagement he looked forward to.

"It does seem pretty callous scheduling," he observed, "to put in a Schools Matinee on the second day of the run."

"Bums on seats, love." John B. Murgatroyd's voice had now taken on Gavin Scholes' slightly ineffectual tone. "Need the money, I'm afraid. Being a set text, you know, we can really cram them in for this show."

None of the cast had thought much of the prospect of doing two shows on the Wednesday. Indeed, the Equity representative in the company had got quite heavy about it, citing any number of rules and regulations against the scheduling. But of course it had been billed for a long time, the seats had been sold to schools from a wide area, and there was very little that could be done about it.

Charles looked with dissatisfaction at the scar on his face and applied another trickle of blood. Not really very good. But the best he could do if he was going to have to whip it off and appear as an unwounded Sewer in Act One Scene Seven. Hmm, maybe if someone in the company was going up to London, they could buy him a stick-on rubber scar. Trouble with those is you have to match the make-up around them so carefully . . .

"Ping-ping-ping," said John B. Murgatroyd suddenly.

"What's that for?"

Back into Felicia's voice for the reply. "Sorry, just the alarm on the old body-clock. Telling me I need a little sustenance." John B. reached into his shoulder bag which lay on the floor, and produced a pewter hip-flask. He unscrewed it and proffered the bottle to Charles.

The head was nobly shaken. A saint, not an ordinary man, thought Charles in wry self-congratulation.

"Well, please yourself," said John B. in his own voice. "I don't think I could get through a Schools Matinee without a few shots of this."

Charles watched in a long pang of envy as his friend raised the bottle to his lips and swallowed.

"Sounds fairly rowdy already," Charles observed, referring to the noise which came from the dressing room Tannoy. Actors all know the familiar buzz of a pre-performance audience, indistinguishable conversations and muffled movements from the stage microphones by the curtain. But the noise from a Schools Matinee is completely different in quality, much higher in pitch and with more giggling and movement. Most of the movement is caused by last-minute changes of seating arrangements, as boys jockey for positions next to the girls they would most like to sit in the dark with, and every child tries to avoid the awful ignominy of sitting next to the teacher.

The lot who were filling the Pinero auditorium that afternoon sounded louder than the average, and that did not augur well for the company.

157

"What lines do you reckon are going to get them going?" asked Charles.

"The giggles? Hmm." John B. gave the question serious consideration. "Well, the Witches'll certainly get a few titters. I'm still not sure Gavin's right to be playing them with lesbian overtones . . . And when George and Felicia kiss in Act One Scene Five, that'll start the usual whistles and catcalls. Individual lines . . . ? Well, the obvious words'll trigger reactions. 'Come to my woman's breasts . . .' Ooh, and if they're paying attention, George should get a boffo when he sees the line of kings in the Apparition Scene."

Charles supplied the relevant quotation. "'And some I see That two-fold balls and treble sceptres carry.'"

"Exactly. They'll like 'two-fold balls'. And George should get a goody on 'The devil damn thee black, thou cream-faced loon!'"

"Do you think I'm going to get anything on the Drunken Porter?"

John B. shook his head firmly. "No chance. What, on a Shakespearean comic character, with schoolkids? Forget it. Well," he then conceded generously, "suppose you might get a tickle on the word 'urine', but that's all. Mind you, could get something on your first entrance . . ."

"As the Porter?"

"No, Bleeding Sergeant. 'What bloody man is that?' Should be good for a giggle."

"Hmm. I think Felicia's going to get the biggest laugh. Wonder how she'll cope with it . . . ?" Charles mused.

"Which line?"

"'I have given suck.'"

"Ooh, yes." John B. giggled with relish. "Yes, particularly the way she delivers it. With that long pause afterwards, I don't think even the slowest schoolboy mind could miss the ambiguity."

Charles felt a moment of conscience. "Do you think we should tip her off? Then she could hurry the line through."

"No way." John B. looked professionally affronted. "Don't be such a wet blanket."

"Trouble is, John B., I know what I'm like. Once we start getting those sort of laughs, I begin to break up. Giggle through the whole show."

"Of course. But that's what matinees are *for*, aren't they?"

"Later in the run, maybe."

"No, right from the start." John B. Murgatroyd shook his head like a parent whose son has just been caught smoking cannabis behind the school cycle-sheds. "Honestly, Charles, since you've given up the booze, you've got really prissy."

To reinforce his point, he took another infuriatingly slow swig from the hip-flask.

At that moment the dressing-room door opened to admit Gavin Scholes. As if by magic, the hip-flask disappeared into the folds of Lennox's brocaded gown.

"Oh, Charles," said the director. "Just a note I forgot to give you yesterday."

Was it imagination, or did Gavin really seem to be avoiding his eye?

"Yes? Which character is this a note for?"

"Apparition of an Armed Head."

"Right, I'm now thinking Apparition of an Armed Head."

"Last night from out front it looked as if you had been waiting in the cauldron all evening."

"What do you mean?"

"Well, your head sort of came up tentatively."

"You try not being tentative on that trap-door platform. It's very unstable. Particularly when you're not allowed to show your torso, because that's still dressed as the Third Murderer."

"But it looked as if you were holding on to the sides."

"You bet I was holding on to the sides. Bloody dangerous with that thing if you don't."

"Well, could you try it not holding on?"

Charles looked dubious.

"Oh, go on, just for this afternoon. Please. Must dash."

As the director hurried out of the dressing room, Charles felt a little cold tremor run down his back.

It was a riotous performance, for the audience at least. Every line John B. Murgatroyd had predicted got its laugh, and a good few others did as well. The audience of schoolchildren, confident that their teachers could not identify them individually in the dark, settled down to have a good time. Having early on decided that the cause of that good time was not going to be Shakespeare's great drama, they enjoyed every ambiguity the text offered.

The company could not be immune to what was happening in the auditorium and, again as John B. had predicted, they became very giggly and undisciplined. George Birkitt seemed unworried by all this; perhaps all his years of television sit coms had led him to expect laughs in whatever role he played. But, for Felicia Chatterton, to judge from the tight scribble of lines between her brows, it was a very trying experience.

Charles Paris didn't enjoy the performance, either. Two anxieties preoccupied him as he ran through his repertoire of parts.

First, he was worried about the imminent interview with Detective Inspector Dowling.

And, second, he was worried that Gavin Scholes wanted to ensure that that interview did not take place.

Charles reasoned it thus. If, as he was coming increasingly to believe, the director had killed Warnock Belvedere, and if, as their conversation of the previous evening suggested, Gavin was afraid Charles had witnessed that crime, then the obvious course was to eliminate the witness before his follow-up interview with Detective Inspector Dowling. Which logic did nothing to put Charles at his ease.

So he was very wary throughout the Schools Matinee. He was uncomfortably aware of the number of potential murder methods a theatre offered. Scenery could fall on people. They could be "assisted" down flights of stairs. And of course

Macbeth demanded a whole armoury of swords and daggers. With so much lethal hardware around, and with much of the action played in half-light, it was no surprise that ugly stories of fatal accidents had built up around the play.

And then there was the trap-door. In rehearsal John B. Murgatroyd had demonstrated that the apparatus could at least give someone a nasty jolt. Charles wondered uneasily whether it could be doctored to cause more permanent damage.

There was no sign of Gavin as Charles, in his coal-scuttle helmet, moved cautiously towards the wooden framework under the stage. The usual Assistant Stage Manager stood by to operate the mechanism, and looked curious as Charles inspected the ropework.

"What's the matter?" the boy hissed.

"Just double-checking," Charles hissed back.

"It's okay."

"Did Gavin give you any notes on the trap-door?"

"Said I should bring you up faster."

"Well, ignore the note. I'm quite happy with the speed I have been going."

"Look, if Gavin said—"

But above them the three Witches were chanting,

"'Come high or low,
Thyself and office deftly show.'"

With a silent prayer, Charles mounted the platform. He took a firm hold on the sides of the cradle, and closed his eyes as he felt the platform surge beneath him.

There was a sudden sharp pain in his knuckles as he broke through the stage and they were barked against the edge of the trap's opening.

In the moment of pain he forgot to crouch.

The Apparition of an Armed Head burst through the bubbling dry ice vapour in the cauldron, with its helmet askew, and rose to reveal its Third Murderer costume underneath. One agonized hand was clutched in its armpit, and from its lips emerged the involuntary word "Shit!"

The Schools Matinee audience were loud in their appreciation of the best bit of Shakespeare they'd ever seen.

He didn't know. Certainly he'd never held on so tight to the cradle before, so maybe that was why he had barked his knuckles. Alternatively, the apparatus might have been booby-trapped (though, fortunately, inadequately booby-trapped).

All he did know was that he was going to keep his eyes skinned for the rest of the performance.

And he would be very relieved when the fights were over.

Charles had more costumes than the other actors in his dressing room, and, since some of his changes were so quick they had to take place in the wings, it took him a little while to collect up all his belongings after the performance. This was a chore that should have been done by Wardrobe, but he didn't have much confidence in the girl with orange-streaked hair, and preferred to be responsible for his own stuff. Nothing worse for an actor than suddenly to find he hasn't got the right pair of trousers in the middle of a quick change.

So, by the time he got back to his dressing room after the Schools Matinee, its other residents had already doffed their armour and rushed to get out of the theatre for a break before the evening show.

Charles was hanging up his costumes on a long, wheeled rack, when he heard the door open behind him.

He turned sharply to see Gavin Scholes. The director was breathing heavily, and looked flustered and upset.

"Oh, Charles. Others all gone?"

"Yes."

It was then that Charles noticed Gavin was carrying the sword used by Macbeth in his final fight.

Chapter Seventeen

STILL, GAVIN SCHOLES seemed to be avoiding Charles's eye. "Charles, I have something to ask you . . ."

"Yes?" He spoke casually, but he was carefully assessing the distance between him and the sword which he had so recently seen carried in the service of both Malcolm and Macbeth.

"I don't like doing it, but I'm afraid I've made a ghastly cock-up . . ."

"Oh yes? What?"

The tension was great, but the bathos was greater.

"Look, I'd completely forgotten, but when I set up this matinee, I agreed with one of the teachers that I'd lead a discussion of the play afterwards. With the cast."

"Oh."

"And I've just bumped into the bloke and he's reminded me about it, and I've dashed back here and everyone else seems to have gone. So I'm sorry, Charles, but would you mind coming and talking to them?"

"No. No problem. Have I got time to get out of costume?"

Gavin grimaced. "Sorry. I've kept them waiting some time already."

"Okay. Don't worry. Just one thing, Gavin," Charles asked, "why have you got that sword?"

"Oh, give them something to look at. There's sure to be a question about whether or not the swords are real."

Charles felt relieved. But he still kept his distance from Gavin as they left the dressing room.

In the passage outside, another shock awaited him. The door to the liquor store-room, on which a new padlock had been fixed, was open. Inside, Norman Phipps could be seen, piling up crates of bottles.

Outside, watching him, stood Detective Inspector Dowling. The policeman turned at the sound of the dressing-room door. "Ah, Mr Paris. I was just having another look at the scene of the . . . er, accident. Are you ready for our little chat?"

Charles explained about the discussion. Gavin endorsed how important it was that Charles should participate.

"Fine," said the Detective Inspector blandly. "It'll keep for half an hour. May I use your office again, Mr Scholes?"

"Of course."

"See you up there when you're ready, Mr Paris."

The discussion was predictable. The boys of only one school had stayed to talk about the play, and clearly they had done so not of their own volition, but because their teacher had told them to.

The boys were also disappointed to see the director accompanied on the stage by only one member of the cast. And, though the range of that member's performance had encompassed the Bleeding Sergeant, the Sewer, the Drunken Porter, the Old Man, the Third Murderer, the Apparition of an Armed Head, the English Doctor, the Scottish Doctor, and soldiers fighting on both sides in the final battle, they did not disguise the fact that they would rather have seen George Birkitt, whom they knew from the telly, or Felicia Chatterton, who was dead dishy.

Gavin gave a brief exposition of his view of the play, which seemed to engage his audience's attention no more than had the actual performance, and then invited questions.

The response was sluggish and only heavy prompting from their teacher, a small, enthusiastic man with gold-rimmed glasses and a wispy beard, elicited anything.

The first question was the one Gavin had anticipated about real swords, and, with a knowing look to Charles, he produced Macbeth's weapon from the wings. He then asked if any of them would like to look at it. This was unwise, because it precipitated a rush on to the stage. The sword was snatched from him and brandished dangerously by a series of small hands before order was re-imposed by the teacher.

"If you've got real weapons," asked a grumpy voice from the front row, "why didn't the fights look more realistic?"

"Oh, I thought they were quite realistic," Gavin objected defensively.

This was greeted by a chorus of derision. "No way", "They were pathetic", "I could do it tons better", "No, they were missing each other by miles" and "*The A-Team*'s much better" came from various parts of the auditorium.

"Yeah." The grumpy voice from the front row added a supplementary question. "Why isn't *Macbeth* more like *The A-Team*?"

This enquiry was greeted with considerable enthusiasm and seemed to be the cue for a series of machine-gun noises and Mr T impressions.

"Well," said Gavin as the hubbub subsided, "I think this is one that perhaps Charles can answer better than I can."

You bastard, thought Charles, as he scraped the bottom of his mind for something to say. He had at least heard of *The A-Team*, thank God. When he had last seen his grandsons, Juliet's boys (which, he realized with horror, had been nearly six months previously), they had talked of nothing else.

"Um, well, you see, what you have to remember is that, for the people of Shakespeare's time, there was no television. Plays were their television, if you like."

"Cor, give me *Eastenders* any day," came an opinion from the back of the auditorium.

Charles persevered. "So for them, you see, the theatre provided everything. Tragedy, comedy . . ."

"Where's the comedy?" demanded an aggressive recently broken voice.

"Well, even in *Macbeth*, there's comedy."

"Where?"

"The Drunken Porter. He's a comic character."

"But he's not *funny*."

"No, I know he's not *funny*, but he is a comic character."
Dear, oh dear, this is uphill work, thought Charles. How on
earth does Frances manage to be a teacher, doing this every day?
"You see, for people of Shakespeare's time, the Porter was
making very good jokes." He parroted this opinion because he
had heard it so often stated, but he couldn't really bring himself
to believe it. "You see, you have the latest sit com, but in the
same way the people of Shakespeare's time had the Drunken
Porter. You have *The A-Team*, they had *Macbeth*."

"Poor sods," said a voice from the back.

The short bearded teacher leapt up in fury. "Who said that?
Come on, who said it? We are not leaving this theatre until the
boy who said that word owns up."

Oh God, thought Charles. We could be here all night.

"Now, come on, I don't care what language you use at home,
but when you're in my charge, you don't use those kind of
words. What will Mr Scholes and Mr . . . er . . . the other
gentleman think of you?"

"I don't think they'll actually mind," said an earnest owl-
faced boy sitting near the teacher. "I think they're probably
used to it. I mean, when that one . . ." He pointed at Charles
". . . popped out of the pot, he said 'Shit'."

This was greeted by choruses of "Yes, he did", "Protheroe's
right, sir", "He really did, he said 'Shit'" and "Did
Shakespeare write that?" Once again it was a while before a
relative calm was re-established.

"Any further questions?" asked the bearded teacher, glaring
round the auditorium.

The owl-faced boy raised his hand. "Yes, sir, please, sir," he
asked with the same unsmiling earnestness.

"Right, Protheroe, what's your question?"

"Well, sir, it's about that bit with the pot."

"Cauldron, Protheroe."

"What, sir?"

"It's called a cauldron."

166

"What is, sir?"

"The pot, Protheroe."

"Oh yes, sir, right, sir. Well . . . when all those people popped out of the pot . . ."

"Yes?" Gavin Scholes smiled encouragingly at the boy.

"Were the Witches going to eat them?"

"I'm sorry?"

"That's my question—were the Witches cannibals?"

"Don't be stupid, Protheroe." The teacher's hand reached round to clip the boy's ear.

"But I wasn't being stupid, sir. I really meant it. It was a serious—ow!"

The teacher rode over a chorus of "Ooh, you hit Protheroe"s and turned to address the two figures on the stage.

"I must apologize for the stupidity of some of my pupils. But I would like to say . . ." At this point he reached into his pocket and produced a file card scribbled with notes. Oh no, Charles groaned inwardly, speeches. "I would like to say how much we appreciate having had this opportunity of talking to you about the . . . er . . ." He heavily italicized the next words ". . . *nuts and bolts* of production. We realize that you are all . . . er, both . . . busy people, and we do appreciate you giving up your time to give us a *glimpse backstage*. As Head of English, I am aware that I can talk about a play until I'm blue in the face—and I'm sure some of my pupils present today reckon I do . . ." He waited for reaction, but his charges were too familiar with his jokes to bother to give him any. "Be that as it may . . ." For a moment he lost his place in his notes. "Be that as it may, yes . . . Yes, well, I can talk about a play till I'm blue in the face, but I'm sure the boys learn a hundred times more by actually seeing the play in production. I sometimes think the best way for them to get to know *Macbeth* is for us actually to mount a school production, but unfortunately, with Mr Palmer currently *locked* into rehearsal for *Joseph and his Amazing Technicolour Dreamcoat*, that is not logistically possible." He lost his way. "Be that as it may . . . And it is . . . I would like, finally . . ." Thank

God, thought Charles ". . . er, finally, to thank Mr Scholes and Mr . . . er . . ." The teacher glanced down at his programme ". . . Mr Murgatroyd . . ." Huh, thought Charles, so much for all my finely differentiated character work ". . . for giving up their time and leading such a stimulating discussion. So, boys . . ." He turned back towards the auditorium ". . . I would be grateful if you could show your appreciation in the usual way."

With three rousing "Hip hip"'s, he wrung three limp "Hooray"'s from the boys, who immediately started to shuffle out of the auditorium, and the discussion was over.

Charles watched Gavin warily as they left the stage, but the director did not seem too interested in him. "Thanks very much for your help, Charles. I must go and sort a few things out in the office."

"Well, if Dowling's up there, tell him I'm on my way."

"Oh, I'd forgotten about him," said Gavin casually, as he set off up the auditorium.

Charles wondered if that could possibly be true.

He changed back into his ordinary clothes and left his dressing room. Through the open door of the store-room, he could still see Norman reorganizing his supplies of drink. It seemed months to Charles since he had discovered Warnock Belvedere's beer-sodden body there, but he knew grimly that he was about to relive that experience in an interview that could prove to be very uncomfortable.

He slipped through a pass-door into the theatre foyer and was about to start up the stairs towards Gavin's office when he caught sight of movement through the glass doors at the front of the theatre.

The bearded schoolmaster was tetchily herding his recalcitrant charges into a minibus.

But it was what was printed on the side of the minibus that caught Charles's attention.

And it brought instantly to his mind another possible solution to the mystery of Warnock Belvedere's death.

Chapter Eighteen

CHARLES RUSHED BACK into the theatre foyer as the school minibus drove away. At the foot of the stairs stood Detective Inspector Dowling. "On my way up to Mr Scholes' office. Care to join me?"

"Just a sec. Must just sort out something at the Box Office."

The detective cocked an ironical eyebrow at him. "A more sensitive man, Mr Paris, might think you were trying to avoid him."

"Only take a minute, I promise."

Dowling glanced at his watch. "Very well. See you up there." And he started up the stairs.

Charles looked through the window of the Box Office to confirm who was on duty, but he went through the pass-door out of the foyer and entered the small room by its back door.

Sandra Phipps looked round in surprise. She sat there, queen of her domain, theatre plans spread over the telephones on the counter in front of her. Behind her were rows of wooden pigeon-holes, each with its stock of different-coloured tickets and its date neatly printed on the frame.

"Charles. What do you want? If it's about comps, you should come to the window, you know."

She looked tired. The defiant brassiness was still there, but under their make-up, her eyes sagged. Her shoulders, under the tight satin of her blouse, drooped.

"I know," said Charles. "It's not about comps."

"Oh?"

"It's about Stewart."

Panic flashed in her eye. "Is he all right?" Sandra asked.

"Yes, he's fine." She slumped with relief. "Or at least he's not fine, is he?"

"What do you mean?"

"Well, he's not gone to school today, has he?"

"No. Tonsillitis."

"Stayed at home."

"Yes. He often gets it. Look, Charles, what is this? What are you on about?"

Before he could answer, the phone rang.

Sandra answered it. "Pinero Theatre Box Office."

She took the booking punctiliously, shuffling her plans to check availability, offering a range of prices, repeating the details of the caller's credit card.

When the call was over, she turned back to Charles. "*Macbeth*'s booking very well. Seems like Gavin's got a success on his hands. Of course, George is a good telly name . . ." Charles said nothing, as she reached round to the relevant pigeon-hole and withdrew a book of tickets, from which she tore two, carefully checking the printed details. "What I really need," she continued, "is to have this whole system computerized. But of course that's money, and . . ."

She seemed to realize that this babbling was not getting her anywhere. She looked straight at Charles. "What is this about Stewart?"

"Just a pity that he should be ill today. When St. Joseph's had a trip to see *Macbeth*."

Sandra shrugged. "Yes, it's bad luck. But the run's only just started. Be plenty of other opportunities to see the show. I'm sure I can slip him in."

"I don't think you will, though, Sandra. Will you?"

She flushed as she looked up at him.

"What do you mean?"

"I've just been talking to Stewart's form teacher."

"Oh?"

"He's the Head of English at the school."

"I know that," she snapped.

"Which is why he led the school party to the play."

"So . . . ?"

"He said in the after-show discussion that he thought his pupils would learn more by seeing the play than by any amount of talking about it."

"Look, it's very good of you to take my son's education so much to heart. I *will* ensure that he sees the play at some point. Will that satisfy you or would you rather—?"

Charles cut through her heavy sarcasm. "Stewart's form teacher also said how much he thought his pupils would learn by actually being in a production of the play . . ."

Sandra avoided his eye. "Well, yes, I'm sure they would, but I don't see what—"

"And yet you say he stopped Stewart from taking part."

"Yes. The understanding was, right from the start, that Stewart could do it, so long as his work didn't suffer. Unfortunately, because the rehearsal schedule got out of hand, he missed some homework and . . ." She gestured helplessly ". . . that was it."

"I see." Charles let her relax for a moment before continuing, "Except that Stewart's form teacher gives a completely different version of events."

"What?"

"He says he never made any fuss about Stewart's work. He didn't care a great deal. He reckoned a boy who wasn't basically academic was going to learn more about *Macbeth* by being in the production as Macduff's Son than by writing any number of essays about it. He said he didn't care how much time Stewart needed to have off for rehearsals."

"Well then, he's changed his tune. He told me—"

"No, he didn't. You told him. He didn't ring you over the weekend after the first runthrough. You rang him, and said that the rehearsals were proving too much for Stewart, that he was getting overtired, and you thought it was your duty, as his mother, to pull him out of the show."

"Well, all right, what if I did?"

A tap on the glass in front of her drew her attention. "Excuse me. Do you have two tickets for this Saturday's matinee? They will be at Senior Citizen rates."

She concentrated once again on her charts and dealt with the booking. Her voice retained its customary professional cheer, but from behind her, Charles could see the flush spreading to her neck.

When the Senior Citizens had departed with their tickets, she turned back to him.

"All right, so I thought the show was too much for Stewart. That was my judgement as his mother. What's wrong with that?"

"If that was the case, why did you tell Gavin it was the school that objected?"

"I thought it sounded better. If I said it was just me, Gavin would have tried to persuade me."

Charles nodded. "Good. But not, I'm afraid, good enough."

"What are you suggesting?"

"I'm suggesting that tiredness wasn't the reason you wanted Stewart out of the production. I'm suggesting that there was something about this production of *Macbeth* that upset your son. That still upsets him, which is why he suddenly developed tonsillitis this morning, so that he didn't have to come and see it."

"I don't know what you're talking about."

"But I do."

And he did. Suddenly, he saw what had happened with dazzling clarity. It was all in the play. Think about Gavin Scholes' production of *Macbeth* and it all became clear.

Charles had observed before that nearly everyone was involved in the battle scenes. Even Lady Macduff and the Witches had to change sex and don armour. So once the battle scenes started, almost all the company would be milling round the stage area, and the dressing room area would be virtually deserted.

As it had been at the end of the first Saturday runthrough.

172

In fact, there would only have been three people in the dressing room area.

Felicia Chatterton, having given her all in the Sleepwalking Scene, would be lying on her dressing-room floor doing relaxation exercises.

That left two.

Warnock Belvedere, who had refused to double, had been there since the end of Act One Scene Six.

And Stewart Phipps, good-looking thirteen-year-old Stewart Phipps, had been there since Charles and the other Murderers had killed him in Act Four Scene Two.

"I think, Sandra, that what upset Stewart about this production of *Macbeth* was that Warnock Belvedere made a pass at him."

The panic in her eyes told him that his guess had been right.

"And I think that that is the reason why Warnock Belvedere was murdered."

All of the colour drained from Sandra Phipps' face.

Chapter Nineteen

NORMAN PHIPPS WAS still reorganizing his store-room when Charles Paris found him. The actor looked at the tubes from the beer kegs and gas cylinders. All had been replaced and looked as good as new. There was no sign that this was the place where one elderly actor had met his untimely, but universally welcomed, demise.

Norman looked up and nodded a greeting. He avoided words whenever they weren't strictly necessary.

"Norman, I've just been talking to Sandra . . ."

"Oh yes?"

"About Stewart and what happened."

Norman deliberately placed another crate on top of a pile. "How do you mean —what happened?" he asked evenly.

"About Warnock Belvedere."

The Bar Manager froze for a split second before asking, "What about Warnock Belvedere?"

"About how he died."

"I thought we knew that. Asphyxiation from the carbon dioxide."

"Yes, but what caused it?"

Norman gave a little shrug. "He was drunk, wasn't he?"

"On a bottle of Courvoisier."

"On top of what he'd had in the bar, yes. Surprising the drink alone didn't kill him."

"Hmm. The question is—where did he get that Courvoisier from?"

Norman looked Charles straight in the eye. "Police seem to reckon he got it out of this cupboard. After he'd broken in here."

"I think he had it before he broke in here."

"Seems unlikely." Still there was no change in the man's even intonation.

"I know he had it before he broke in here," said Charles.

"Oh. How's that?"

"I saw him when I came down from the bar at closing time." Norman Phipps again saved words, but said it all with a sceptically raised eyebrow.

"Yes, I know I was pissed, but not that pissed. He was definitely holding a bottle, and he said it had been given him by a 'generous friend'."

"Afraid I didn't know any of his friends," said Norman, turning back to his pile of crates.

"There was another suspicious thing about the death." Charles waited for a reaction, but didn't get it. "When I found Warnock's body in here, the light was switched off."

Again, the momentary freeze before Norman said, "So what?"

"It seems unlikely that he switched the light out before conveniently passing out on the floor."

"Possible."

"But, as I say, unlikely."

A non-committal shrug.

"Norman, Sandra says she gave Warnock that bottle of brandy."

This, at last, did produce a reaction. Norman's body went rigid; then he turned slowly to face Charles. To the latter's surprise, on the Bar Manager's face was a smile of pleasure. "Did she?" he asked softly.

"Yes. She did. Which would suggest very strongly that she was responsible for Warnock's death."

Norman Phipps shook his head slowly. "No," he said. "She's lying."

But he didn't say the words as if they were important. The feeling of pleasure still meant more to him. As a casual afterthought, he added, "Sandra didn't kill him. I did."

175

"Because of what he did to Stewart?"

A slow nod of the head. "Yes. I wouldn't have done it. I thought Stewart would just get over the experience, in time. I mean, I agreed he should come out of the production, but that was all. Not enough for Sandra, though. I suppose she was feeling guilty. She should have been keeping an eye on him. That's what a chaperon in the theatre's for, isn't it?"

Charles nodded. "Yes, to protect children from people like Warnock . . . amongst other things."

"Hmm." Norman spoke as if in a dream. "Anyway, Sandra went on so, I had to do something . . ."

So Charles had been right. It was like *Macbeth*, the woman urging the man to murder. But he had got the personnel wrong. Not Felicia Chatterton and Russ Lavery, but Sandra and Norman Phipps.

It all fitted. Even, he thought, ironically, down to Duncan being murdered by his host. Hadn't Warnock always insisted on addressing Norman as "Mine Host"?

"So what you mean is that Sandra told you to kill him?"

"No. It wasn't like that."

"How was it then?" asked Charles Paris gently.

The Bar Manager came out of his reverie and focused on his interrogator. "Not a great marriage, Sandra and me. Doesn't look that good from the outside, does it? Afraid it's not that much better from the inside. Fact is, we're . . . different. Sandra's more . . . what's the word? Passionate? Physical?"

"I see."

"Yes, I bet you do. What I mean is, in crude terms, she likes sex more than I do. I don't mind it once in a while, but . . ." He shrugged.

"So the alibi she gave the police . . . ?"

He let out a short bark of laughter. "Just getting at me. Again."

"Like she got at you over Stewart?"

Norman Phipps nodded. "She went on and on about it. Said

that an experience like that, at that age, would make a boy homosexual for life . . ."

Now it was Charles's turn to be quiet. He didn't want to break the intimacy of the confessional.

"I said I thought he'd get over it, and then she said . . . she said . . ." His voice did not break, but he seemed to be having physical difficulty in getting the words out. "She said that he'd grow up like his father. She implied that the reason I didn't like sex as much as she did was that I was . . . that I wasn't a real man . . ."

His voice stopped again, but still his manner remained unemotional.

"She said a real man wouldn't let someone like Warnock get away with doing something like that to his son."

"So you thought you'd show her?" Charles prompted gently. "Show her that Warnock hadn't got away with it?"

A slow "Yes" and a nod. "It wasn't difficult. I'd thought about the carbon dioxide many times before. I once nearly passed out down here when I was fixing that electrical socket." He pointed to the bottom of the wall. "There was a leak from one of the cylinders. I knew what was happening, so I just got out. But, even at the time, I remember wondering what it would be like for someone who was already unconscious.

"You're right, of course, I had got the bottle out earlier. Just left it on the table in his dressing room."

"But how did you know he'd stay in the theatre? He might have taken the bottle back to his digs."

"I went down just after closing time. I . . ." For the first time, the voice was choked with emotion. "I told him that . . . that Stewart had liked what he'd done. I said Stewart wanted to see him again. I said, if he waited in the dressing room, I'd . . . bring Stewart to him."

That fitted. Charles remembered Warnock's unwholesome desire for a "nice little bumboy". He also remembered with distaste that the old actor had even propositioned *him*. So, with Norman's offer of his son, and a bottle of brandy to while away the time, Warnock would happily wait in his dressing room.

"I went home with Sandra usual time. I waited an hour, then came back to the theatre. I've got keys, you know."

"Was Sandra asleep?"

"Just about. She doesn't sleep well."

Lady Macbeth again, thought Charles.

"As I had hoped, the old bastard was out cold. I took his stick and used it to break the locks. Then I dragged him in, laid him on his face and put the empty bottle in his hand."

"Did you wear gloves?"

Norman shook his head. "I've handled everything in this room. Nothing odd to find my prints on the bottle. And there would be plenty of his.

"Then I broke the beer tubes and the gas lines. I closed the door, to make doubly sure the CO_2 wouldn't escape, and waited."

"How long?"

"Twenty minutes. When I opened the door, the job was done."

"So then you made your one mistake by switching off the light, and went back home?"

"That's it. Sandra was awake when I got back, worried where I'd been. I told her what I'd done, but she . . . she . . ." Once again emotion threatened. ". . . she didn't react like I'd hoped . . ."

The murderer turned away, and rubbed the back of his hand noisily against his nose. When he turned back, he asked pathetically, "But she really did say she'd given him the bottle of brandy?"

"Yes, she did."

Norman Phipps let out a sigh. Again, the information seemed to comfort him. Perhaps it proved that, beneath the jagged surface of their marriage, his wife really did feel some love for him.

"Mr Paris . . ."

Charles turned guiltily at the sound of the voice behind him.

Detective Inspector Dowling stood framed in the doorway. There was no longer any diffidence in his manner; on his face was an expression of uncompromising anger. "You're not going to be able to hide from me, Mr Paris."

"Oh, I wasn't trying to. I just . . ." Charles felt himself blushing. Why did he always revert to a guilty adolescent when faced by an authority figure?

"I've had enough faffing around, Mr Paris," the Detective Inspector continued. "I want to ask you some serious questions about the murder of Warnock Belvedere."

Oh, thought Charles in panic, so the police know it was murder. Oh God, and I'm still their main suspect and they're bound to—

But his illogical ramblings were interrupted by a voice from the other side of the room.

"I think, Detective Inspector," said Norman Phipps quietly, "that I'm the one you want to talk to."

Chapter Twenty

IT WAS THE following Wednesday's Schools Matinee, and the buzz from the auditorium on the dressing-room Tannoy sounded even more hectic than the week before.

"This lot's going to be trouble," said John B. Murgatroyd, his voice strangely muffled inside his helmet.

"Why are you wearing that bloody thing?" asked Charles.

"Protection, laddie, protection. Filter the beer fumes emanating from your gob, me old chum."

Charles giggled weakly. Shouldn't have gone into the bar at lunchtime. Fatal. He knew that, really. And shouldn't have had three pints. Would have a desperate urge to pee in the middle of the Apparition Scene. Oh dear, wouldn't do to pee in the Witches' cauldron.

Still, it was only a Schools Matinee.

His pledge had lasted till after the previous Wednesday's second show, but no longer. Well, he had promised himself a drink once he'd worked out who'd killed Warnock Belvedere. In fact, in all the relief of ceasing to be a murder suspect, it'd been a good few drinks.

And the familiar dry ache of a hangover had greeted him on the Thursday morning. It hurt, but it certainly felt more normal. Felicia Chatterton might go on about her body-clock, but Charles Paris had one too, and his had been thrown seriously out of kilter by those eight days without the regular imperatives of licensing hours.

Eight days. Not bad. Damned nearly nine days. At least, he could prove he could do it. Drink? Well, I can take it or leave it, he would now be able to say with confidence. But he wouldn't leave it again for a while.

Well over a week, though. Pretty good. Well over the week that he'd promised himself he would announce to Frances as a proof of his reformed character.

The trouble was, he hadn't got round to ringing her during the period of actual abstinence, and to ring her and speak of it retrospectively wouldn't have quite the same dramatic effect.

No, he'd have to think of another approach. He would ring her soon. Really.

"Saw some of the kids coming in." John B. Murgatroyd's muffled voice brought him back to reality. "Looked a right load of scruffs. Yes, I think they're going to be trouble. Still, Gavin's away," he added innocently.

There wasn't much comfort for Charles in the director's absence. Gavin was in London auditioning for his production after next, Alan Ayckbourn's *Ten Times Table*. He was already into rehearsal for *Deathtrap*, the second show of the season. And he hadn't drawn Charles aside for a little chat about either play. So it looked as if Maurice Skellern's optimism about "other parts" had been misplaced. Once *Macbeth* finished its run, it was going to be back to London, with all the delights of his bedsitter and the Lisson Grove Unemployment Office, for Charles Paris.

Oh well, wouldn't be the first time.

And at least Russ Lavery had been kept on to play the young man in *Deathtrap*. Good part for someone so new to the business. That boy will go far, thought Charles, with only a twinge of jealousy.

John B. Murgatroyd reached into the folds of his Lennox gown and produced the hip-flask. This time Charles accepted his offer.

"Settle the beer," he said, somehow making the whisky sound like a medical necessity.

"Five minutes, please," called the Stage Manager's voice over the Tannoy, facing Charles with a dilemma of the bladder. He felt he should have a pee before the show started, but it was more a logical thought than an urgent necessity. And he knew, with that amount of beer inside him, if he had one pee, he'd be peeing all afternoon. Better to keep his nerve and hold it. Sometimes go for hours like that.

On the other hand . . . It would be dreadful to be taken short on stage. He didn't want to add a new legend to the apocrypha of stories of actors peeing into pot-plants, bottles and armour during performances.

Hmm. Tricky one.

He succumbed and had a pee.

As soon as the play started, it was evident that John B. Murgatroyd's assessment of the audience had erred on the side of charity. They were an awful load of little buggers.

They greeted the Witches' first appearance with raucous catcalls, which drowned most of their words. And, predictably enough, Duncan's opening line, "What bloody man is that?" got a huge belter.

The bloody man in question, waiting at the back of the auditorium, felt a tremor pass through Lennox, who was supporting him. "Come on, love," murmured John B. Murgatroyd, and began to steer the Bleeding Sergeant down the aisle.

They would never be absolutely certain, but they both remained convinced to the end of their days that the leg outstretched across the gangway had been deliberately placed. Certainly no planning could have made it more effective. Charles lost his footing and stumbled forward, dragging John B. in his wake.

Their tumbled arrival at the foot of the stage was rewarded by a huge laugh. The audience of schoolchildren settled back. They were going to enjoy this.

Charles was still supported by Lennox, as per rehearsal, when he went through the Bleeding Sergeant's somewhat wordy account of Macbeth and Banquo's battle against "the merciless Macdonwald." At one point he looked full into Lennox's face, and at that moment John B. Murgatroyd closed his eyes.

Charles realized instantly why his friend had kept his helmet on in the dressing room. This joke had taken preparation. Neatly written on the pale make-up of the right eyelid was the word "Fuck"; and on the left eyelid the word "Off".

Charles, who was maundering on about "shipwracking storms and direful thunders", felt his voice begin to tremble as the giggle caught up with him. John B., making it look as if he were helping out his ailing comrade, slapped him on the back and took his hand in a comforting, manly grasp.

Charles felt something hard and round thrust into his hand. Squinting as he tried to continue his lines, he looked down.

There, nestling in his palm, was a walnut.

While being dragged off to have his gashes attended to (moving rather faster than usual because he was desperate for another pee), Charles managed to fall against Donalbain, and as the other actor reached to help him, shoved the walnut into his unsuspecting hand.

From there on, throughout the play it did the rounds, provoking a whole lot of giggling backstage, and a whole lot of new moves onstage, as actors desperately tried to avoid the fate of being the one who had to take the walnut off.

And the audience continued to chatter, whistle and devise other diversionary tactics.

They rustled crisp packets. Then one of them, no doubt a future captain of industry, had the bright idea of blowing them up and bursting them.

In a more planned campaign, a group of them set the alarms of their digital watches to go off at one-minute intervals.

And, meanwhile, the barracking also continued. Many lines took on new and filthy meanings. All the play's dramatic climaxes were defused by heckling.

"'I have done the deed,'" Macbeth announced.

"Ooh, you dirty beast!" came a cry from the audience.

In the Banquet Scene Lady Macbeth's line, "When all's

done, You look but on a stool" was capped by a call of "Well, you should have flushed it, shouldn't you?"

As the Witches loaded their ingredients into the cauldron there were demands for more ketchup.

And so on and so on.

Once that kind of thing starts in a performance, it's difficult to stop, and the cast, relaxed into the second week of their run and secure in the knowledge that Gavin Scholes was in London for the day, made little attempt to stop it.

Mounting hysteria ran through the company. They knew it was unprofessional, they knew they shouldn't. But they did.

Felicia Chatterton alone seemed immune to the general mood. She was incapable of levity and continued, against all the odds, to give her Lady Macbeth.

And it was good. As ever, Charles had to admit that. But he really would like to see her break up on stage. Just once.

He watched her as she drifted about the stage in her low-cut nightgown for the Sleepwalking Scene. Oblivious to the catcalls from the audience, her concentration on the role remained total.

He moved his legs uneasily. Oh God, he couldn't need yet *another* pee, could he? He tried to think of something else.

The Gentlewoman in the scene seemed to be acting closer to him than usual, and as she said the line, "I would not have such a heart in my bosom for the dignity of the whole body", she suddenly tapped Charles on the shoulder.

He started at the unexpected action, and as he turned, felt a familiar object thrust into his hand. The Gentlewoman, backing away downstage, stuck her tongue out at him.

Charles Paris knew he shouldn't, but he couldn't resist it.

He walked across to the sleepwalking Lady Macbeth, and neatly dropped the walnut down her delicious cleavage.

He was rewarded by a look of amazement, and then a sweet, sweet moment as Felicia Chatterton dissolved into uncontrollable giggles.

About the Author

SIMON BRETT is the author of eleven previous Charles Paris theatrical mysteries, a collection of short stories, *Tickled to Death*, and two novels of psychological suspense that have achieved widespread critical praise, *Dead Romantic* and *A Shock to the System*. His most recent mystery was *A Nice Class of Corpse*.